STAR WARS

THE CLONE WARS™

GUARDIANS OF THE CHISS KEY

BY RYDER WINDHAM
COVER ILLUSTRATED BY WAYNE LO
COLORED BY TARA RUEPING

Grosset & Dunlap
An Imprint of Penguin Group (USA) Inc.

LucasBooks

GROSSET & DUNLAP
Published by the Penguin Group
Penguin Group (USA) Inc., 375 Hudson Street, New York, New York 10014, USA
Penguin Group (Canada), 90 Eglinton Avenue East, Suite 700,
Toronto, Ontario M4P 2Y3, Canada
(a division of Pearson Penguin Canada Inc.)
Penguin Books Ltd., 80 Strand, London WC2R 0RL, England
Penguin Group Ireland, 25 St. Stephen's Green, Dublin 2,
Ireland (a division of Penguin Books Ltd.)
Penguin Group (Australia), 250 Camberwell Road, Camberwell, Victoria 3124,
Australia (a division of Pearson Australia Group Pty. Ltd.)
Penguin Books India Pvt. Ltd., 11 Community Centre,
Panchsheel Park, New Delhi—110 017, India
Penguin Group (NZ), 67 Apollo Drive, Rosedale,
Auckland 0632, New Zealand (a division of Pearson New Zealand Ltd.)
Penguin Books (South Africa) (Pty.) Ltd., 24 Sturdee Avenue,
Rosebank, Johannesburg 2196, South Africa

Penguin Books Ltd., Registered Offices:
80 Strand, London WC2R 0RL, England

The book is published in partnership with LucasBooks, a devision of Lucasfilm, Ltd.

ISBN 978-0-448-45745-1   10 9 8 7 6 5 4 3 2 1

ALWAYS LEARNING   **PEARSON**

CHAPTER 1

Eleven years before the Clone Wars . . .

"The pirate ship is coming in fast, Count Dooku!" said the captain of the patrol cruiser. "It was lucky you managed to get a tracking device onto their hull."

"Luck had nothing to do with it, Captain Krempil," replied the Jedi Master, who had a curved-handled lightsaber clipped to his belt. He stood beside his comrade, Jedi Knight Ring-Sol Ambase, on the patrol cruiser's bridge. The one-hundred-and-fifty-meter-long cruiser had a tapered bow that bore the yellow-and-blue insignia of the Malarian Alliance and was nestled in the shadow of a large asteroid at the outer edge of a vast asteroid belt that stretched past a cloudy green nebula. Dooku gestured to the asteroids visible through the main viewport and said, "When you have a visual on the *Random Mallet*, target the primary sensor array."

"Sensor array?" Krempil said with obvious displeasure. "But we could direct all weapons to their engines and blow them clear out of the—"

"No, Captain," Dooku said politely but firmly. "Just the sensor array."

And then the *Random Mallet*, the McGrrrr Gang's battered, hammer-shaped frigate, veered out of the asteroid belt and headed for the nebula. The patrol cruiser dropped out of the asteroid's shadow, sped after the frigate, and fired its laser cannons. The laser bolts struck the fleeing frigate's large sensor array, which blossomed into a bright explosion of fire and twisted metal.

Inside the patrol cruiser, Captain Krempil turned to the two Jedi standing on the bridge and said, "They're making a run for the nebula!"

"We can see that quite clearly, Captain," Dooku replied calmly.

Ring-Sol Ambase, a lean man with silver hair that made him appear almost as old as Dooku, looked past the heads of the cruiser's pilot and navigator to the port side viewport and watched the space pirates' frigate weave past several asteroids before it vanished into the nebula.

"The tracker's no use to us now," Captain Krempil said bitterly. "Our scanners won't work in all that space dust."

"I'm well aware of that, too," Dooku said as he moved behind the navigator's seat. "Bring us to a stop between those asteroids and the edge of the nebula."

The patrol cruiser decelerated and stopped a short distance from the asteroids. Krempil looked at the Jedi and said, "What now? Do we just sit here and wait for the McGrrrr Gang to come out?"

Dooku nodded. "We've already damaged their sensor array, hyperdrive engine, and the starboard directional thrusters. When they grow tired of flying in circles, they'll come out, and then we'll have them."

"What if the McGrrrr Gang doesn't grow tired?"

"They can't stay in the nebula forever, Captain," Ambase said. "Even pirates eventually get hungry."

"I'm not so certain about *these* pirates," Krempil said. "Even without a working hyperdrive, they've managed to evade us for almost three days straight and brought us all the way to the edge of Wild Space. I don't imagine they'll surrender willingly anytime soon."

"I don't expect them to surrender at all," Dooku said, keeping his gaze fixed on the nebula. "They're desperate men. If they can't escape or defeat us, they'll die trying."

Krempil glared at the Jedi. "We had their ship dead in our sights when they left the asteroid belt. Why didn't you let me kill them all when we had the chance?"

Ambase looked at Krempil and said, "The Malarian Alliance requested Jedi assistance to bring the McGrrrr Gang to justice, and we agreed to do that. Jedi only take lives in self-defense or when otherwise defenseless lives are threatened. If the pirates leave us no choice but to destroy their ship, then we shall do what we must."

An alarm chirped from the communication officer's console. The officer switched off the alarm, adjusted her headset, and said, "We're picking up a transmission, Captain. It appears to be originating from just outside the nebula."

Dooku remained at the viewport while Ambase stepped past Krempil and hunkered down over the comm officer's console. Studying the transmission's readout on a sensor scope, Ambase said, "Could it be from the pirates?"

"It doesn't resemble any of their earlier transmissions," the comm officer said. "It sounds like a cross between random noise and atonal music. If it's a language, our computer doesn't recognize it."

"I'd be surprised if the computer *did* recognize it," Dooku said. "After all, we're in uncharted territory. Few Republic ships have ventured this far beyond the Outer Rim."

Ambase pointed to three fluctuations on the sensor scope's readout and said, "Those look like repeat patterns. The transmission is probably an automated recording. Possibly a distress signal."

"Or a warning," Dooku said.

"Or a trap," added Krempil. "The pirates may be trying to distract us."

"I suspect McGrrrr would have tried something less sophisticated," Dooku said. Moving back to the viewport, he returned his gaze to the nebula. He gripped the edge of the viewport's frame as he tilted his head slightly to the pilot and said, "Incoming missile. Divert all energy to deflector shields and hang on."

The pilot had no sooner adjusted the controls for the shields when a thunderous blast rocked the cruiser, tossing Ambase and the crew across the bridge. Ambase sailed over a metal railing and smashed against a bulkhead. The navigational console exploded, and loud alarms began blaring. The pilot tumbled across the deck, grabbed a fire extinguisher, and began spraying down the nav console.

Ambase didn't need to examine any sensors to know the cruiser had been hit by a concussion missile. Then Ambase heard the viewport window make a terrible cracking noise and felt a sudden rush of air tearing at his robes.

"Pressure breach!" shouted the communications officer.

"Evacuate to the life pods!" said Krempil as he stumbled across the bridge.

"Cancel that command, Captain," Dooku said calmly as the escaping air whipped at his robe. While Ambase grabbed a cylindrical tank from a bulkhead and began spraying emergency sealant over a crack in the viewport's window, Dooku moved to an illuminated console and adjusted the controls for the cruiser's energy shields, redirecting the shields over the breached hull as he increased power to the shield strength. The bridge's air pressure stabilized quickly.

"Back to your stations!" Krempil shouted as the pilot put out the fire at the nav console. "Direct all weapons on that frigate!"

Ambase looked through the viewport and saw the *Random Mallet*'s aft thrusters fire and then the *Mallet* rapidly receded toward a distant cluster of stars. "Too late," he said. "The pirates just jumped into hyperspace."

"What?" Krempil said with surprise, but then his face went red with rage. "How?! Their hyperdrive was damaged!"

"Evidently," Dooku said, "they either repaired it or had a backup engine." Turning to consult another sensor scope, he added, "Our tracking device was still on the pirate ship before it escaped. When they exit hyperspace, we'll pick up their trail."

"We're not going anywhere," Krempil fumed, "until I contact my superiors on Namadii. They'll be very disappointed when I tell them about how—"

Another chirp sounded from the comm console. The comm officer said, "It's that unidentified transmission again, sir."

Krempil said, "Probably just an echo from the pirate ship."

Dooku looked through the viewport and said, "I don't believe the McGrrrr Gang is responsible for the transmission, Captain. I surmise it's coming from the spacecraft seventy meters off our port side."

"What?" Krempil looked out the viewport and saw a small, teardrop-shaped spacecraft slowly tumbling across space. The spacecraft had a single, elliptical thruster and a curved, narrow, black slit that appeared to be a window. "It looks like an escape pod," Krempil said. He looked at a data readout on the comm console and added, "Why isn't that pod showing up on our sensors?"

"It must have some kind of frequency jammer," the comm officer said.

As Jedi, both Dooku and Ambase were strong with the Force, an energy field that spanned the entire galaxy. The Force empowered them with great strength and speed and enabled them to lift and move objects without any physical contact. They could perceive their surroundings in ways that ordinary life-forms could not and at times even foretell the future. Drawing from the Force, Dooku said, "I sense a life-form in the spacecraft."

"I sense it, too," Ambase said. Then added, "And . . . it's strong with the Force!"

As the small vessel tumbled past the cruiser, Dooku said, "It's drifting toward the asteroid belt." He turned to the navigator. "Lock a tractor beam onto it."

The navigator consulted a scope as he adjusted the tractor beam controls, then said, "I can't get a lock on anything, sir. The pod is invisible on our sensors, so the tractor won't—"

"Then operate the tractor beam manually," Dooku said impatiently.

"We can't, sir," the navigator said, embarrassed. "The controls are . . . well, they're fully automatic."

Dooku looked at Krempil and said, "Ambase and I require your shuttle."

Krempil raised his eyebrows. "You're going after that pod?"

"Precisely."

"But what about the McGrrrr Gang?"

"We'll go after them later," Dooku said as he and Ambase swept off the bridge.

Dooku steered the box-shaped shuttle after the unidentified vessel, which was visible in the distance, still tumbling toward the asteroids. Seated beside Dooku in the shuttle's cockpit, Ambase familiarized himself with the docking-tube controls as he said, "Let's hope the pod's passenger isn't hostile."

"We don't even know whether the vessel *is* a pod," Dooku said. "It could be a spacious ship, built for a small species. We'll find out soon enough. We should reach it in about a minute. Are you ready to lock on?"

"Yes." Keeping his hand near the docking-tube controls, Ambase said, "Captain Krempil didn't seem very happy to let us borrow this shuttle. He was so eager to go after the McGrrrr Gang, I wouldn't be surprised if he decides to leave without us."

"Krempil is a coward and a fool. He won't go anywhere until we're back on board with him." Dooku shook his head. "It's bad enough that the Galactic Senate expects the Jedi Order to serve politicians, but that we must also answer to paramilitary organizations is insulting."

Ambase glanced at Dooku. "Insulting? Do you mean personally?"

"Not at all," Dooku said as if the thought had never occurred to him. "It's insulting to our ideals. The Jedi Order should serve the will of the Force, not the whims of corrupt bureaucrats. For all we know, helping the Malarian Alliance capture the McGrrrr Gang might end up more disastrous than what happened on Galidraan."

Ambase shook his head. "I still can't believe we lost eleven Jedi in that battle."

"Jedi weren't the only losses," Dooku said. "And all because we believed we were doing the right thing when we went up against those Mandalorians."

"The circumstances were unfortunate."

"No, Ring-Sol. The circumstances were avoidable."

Ambase almost questioned Dooku's comment but decided against it. He and Dooku had been friends for years, and he was well aware of Dooku's concerns and opinions about the Galactic Senate. At the moment, he was more intent on preventing the unidentified vessel's destruction than engaging in a debate.

Dooku expertly guided the shuttle into an orbital path around the teardrop-shaped spacecraft. Testing a switch on the control console in front of him, he said, "The vessel is invisible to the shuttle's tracking sensors, too. We'll have to do this the hard way." He maneuvered the shuttle closer to the vessel.

Ambase eyed the vessel's exterior and said, "That triangular panel must be the hatch. I don't see any external controls or locking mechanisms, but we can . . ." Ambase's head jerked back as he once more sensed the Force's power radiating from the spacecraft. "Do you feel that?"

"Indeed," Dooku said. "The mysterious traveler is as strong with the Force as a Jedi. This day is turning out to be full of surprises."

As the shuttle continued to rotate around the vessel, Ambase deployed the shuttle's docking tube. The tube was still extending from the shuttle when a dark shape slapped against the cockpit's window, surprising Ambase and causing him to accidentally hit the wrong control lever. The docking tube struck the vessel harder than intended, sending it faster toward the asteroids.

"Mynock," Dooku said, identifying the creature with tapered, membranous wings and a large, round mouth that had already suctioned to the outside of the window. Dooku made a sweeping gesture with his fingers as he used the Force to push the energy-eating parasite off the window. The Mynock fell away, leaving an ugly suction mark.

Dooku punched the shuttle's accelerator and raced after the vessel. Ambase saw a wide asteroid looming directly in the vessel's path and said, "Hurry!"

Outside the viewport, distant stars appeared to blur as Dooku banked hard to go after the elusive vessel. As they rapidly neared the wide asteroid, Dooku concentrated his Force powers on the pod to draw it closer to the shuttle while Ambase readjusted the docking-tube controls. The docking tube made a loud *thunk* as it touched the pod's convex hull.

"We have it!" Ambase said.

Dooku sent the shuttle into a steep dive, taking the now-secured vessel with it. They passed so close to the asteroid that the shuttle's sensor systems screeched in protest. As they angled away from the asteroid, Dooku said, "Now that we're attached to the craft, are we getting any readouts?"

Ambase looked at a data display on his console. "The vessel has a pressurized atmosphere that's almost identical with our own. The passenger breathes as we do."

"Evidently," Dooku said as he brought the shuttle to a stop at a safe distance from the asteroids. He activated the comlink, opened a signal to the patrol cruiser, and said, "Dooku to Captain Krempil, Ambase and I will inspect the spacecraft to determine whether the passenger poses any threat. Stand by for my next transmission."

"Yes, Master Dooku," Krempil's sullen voice crackled from the comlink.

Ambase followed Dooku out of the cockpit. Dooku opened the hatch to the passage tube, and they stepped into the airlock. After Ambase sealed the hatch behind them, they proceeded through the tube's next hatch until they stood before the triangular panel that they assumed was the attached spacecraft's egress hatch. Dooku held one hand close to his lightsaber. Ambase did the same as he leaned forward to examine the triangular panel and said, "No visible grips or latches."

"Perhaps the passenger doesn't have dexterous limbs." Dooku moved his left hand around the edges of the panel. Unexpectedly, one edge flickered into a length of soft, white light, and then the panel made a hissing sound as it slid back into the hull, leaving a triangular opening.

Dooku and Ambase gazed into the small

spacecraft. The padded interior consisted of a curved seat that encircled an elevated floor-mounted orb containing small, shimmering lights. Ambase said, "It certainly resembles an escape pod. That orb might be the navigational controls. But where's the life-form? I can still sense its presence."

Dooku stepped into the pod and crouched down below the central orb. He found a large ovoid container that was wedged between the orb's base and the bottom of the seat. The container was roughly seventy-five centimeters long, and its opaque shell appeared to be made of marbled plastic. Reaching out with the Force, Dooku sensed a heartbeat within the container.

"I've found the passenger," Dooku said. "Give me a hand, Ring-Sol."

Ambase moved around Dooku, crawled onto the curved seat, and looked down at the ovoid container. He brushed his fingers over the container, then said, "It's warm."

The Jedi carefully dislodged the container and moved it onto the seat. Before either could ponder how to open the container, two narrow beams of light snaked across its marbled surface, and then the shell opened and unfolded to reveal a sleeping baby, a humanoid male, lying on a thin-cushioned pad with a silver blanket kicked down around his feet. The baby had blue skin and a head topped with glossy, black hair. The baby wriggled, then opened his eyes and looked up at the two Jedi. The baby's eyes were bright red.

"Interesting," Dooku said. "The passenger has dexterous limbs after all. Just very small limbs."

Ambase looked at Dooku and said, "Surely, the Force itself brought the three of us to this place and point in time."

"I wonder," Dooku said, but his tone hinted at doubt.

"How can you be unsure?" Ambase said as he shifted the silver blanket over the baby's legs and small torso. "What are the chances of two Jedi, traveling through an uncharted sector of space, finding a Force-sensitive infant alone in a runaway pod? This is no coincidence, Dooku."

"I never said it was a coincidence. I merely wonder if something other than the Force brought us all here."

"Something else?" Baffled, Ambase said, "What are you implying?"

"Think about it, Ring-Sol. The baby wasn't piloting this pod. Someone *put* him in here, someone with technology that can't be detected by our sensors. Perhaps that same someone was able to determine that the Malarian cruiser carried two Force users and deliberately sent this Force-sensitive baby to us."

"But how could anyone have known we would arrive in this area? We didn't know ourselves until we followed the McGrrrr Gang here."

Dooku gestured to the baby. "We've never encountered this species. Their sensors may be more advanced than ours and might have anticipated our course from many light-years away."

Ambase adjusted the baby's blanket again and spotted a small, glass cylinder near the baby's feet. He picked up the cylinder and saw it contained an arrangement of thin, wirelike filaments, then held it out for Dooku's inspection and said, "This may contain valuable data."

Looking around the pod's interior, Dooku said, "This entire pod is valuable. It's much more than just a spacecraft. It's an introduction to an alien civilization, possibly a key to unlocking another realm of space."

"I suppose we'll find out after we bring the baby and pod back to Coruscant."

Dooku raised his eyebrows. "Perhaps we should first try to locate the baby's homeworld and find out why he was placed in this pod. What if his people are searching for him as we speak?"

"And what if they're not? As you just said, someone may have *sent* the baby to us. And as for finding the baby's origins and identity, our best course of action is to take him and the pod back to the Jedi Temple."

Dooku grimaced. "Would you be so determined to bring the baby to the Jedi Temple if he wasn't Force-sensitive?"

Ambase let out an exasperated sigh. "We can't very well abandon him in the pod or leave him with the Malarian Alliance, and we can't spend forever waiting for someone to claim him, either. He's a *baby*, Dooku. He needs *help*. We need to make sure he's healthy."

The baby made a gurgling sound.

"And we need to feed him," Ambase added. "As for raising him as a Jedi, that's a decision the Jedi Council will have to make."

"Then his fate is sealed," Dooku said ruefully. "He *will* become a Jedi."

Ring-Sol Ambase shook his head. "You confound me, Dooku. You speak as if the baby is condemned."

"Everyone should have the liberty to choose their own path. So long as the Jedi path is paved by the Galactic Senate, we're all condemned."

"You forget we have our honor and traditions."

"I'm not forgetting anything, Ring-Sol. Consider how well our honor and traditions served the Jedi who died on Galidraan." Dooku stepped out of the pod. Ambase followed, carrying the baby.

While another Jedi task force was assigned to help the Malarian Alliance pursue the McGrrrr Gang, Dooku and Ring-Sol Ambase brought the blue-skinned baby boy and his escape pod to the Jedi Temple on the planet Coruscant. At the Jedi

Archives, experts analyzed every part of the escape pod as well as the glass cylinder that Ambase had discovered with the boy.

The escape pod's propulsion system was so completely alien that the experts had to admit they could neither operate nor replicate the technology. The glass cylinder was indeed a data-storage device that held information about the boy, but droid cryptographers and translators were mostly mystified by the data. They concluded that the boy's species called themselves the Chiss, but failed to determine the precise coordinates of Chiss space. Their best guess at the boy's name was Nuru Kungurama.

Just as Dooku anticipated, the twelve members of the Jedi Council agreed that Nuru Kungurama should be raised to become a Jedi. They also decided that the Chiss escape pod should be moved to a storage vault in the Jedi Archives.

Not long after this decision, Dooku stunned the Council when he renounced his commission and left the Jedi Order. He returned to his homeworld, Serenno, where he claimed his birthright as the Count of Serenno and gained immediate access to his wealthy family's fortune.

For several years, Count Dooku's actions and whereabouts were a mystery. Eventually, he reemerged as a political firebrand and rallied thousands of star systems to join his Separatist movement, which threatened to secede from the Senate's government and divide the Galactic Republic. The civil war that ensued became known as the Clone Wars.

Eleven years after the discovery of the Chiss escape pod at the edge of Wild Space, Dooku, Ring-Sol Ambase, and Nuru Kungurama would meet again during the Clone Wars.

CHAPTER 2

Nuru Kungurama said, "Is he still breathing?"

"Talk to me, Chatterbox!" said Knuckles. "Say something!"

A burbling noise came from Chatterbox's mouth, then his head slumped to his left shoulder and he passed out again. Breaker said, "Keep his head and chest elevated."

Chatterbox, Knuckles, and Breaker were Republic Army clone troopers and members of Breakout Squad. They were in one of the docking bays at Bilbringi Depot, a facility on the largest asteroid in the Bilbringi system, along the hyperspace route known as the Namadii Corridor. The only vessel in the docking bay was the wide thirty-meter-long Suwantek Systems TL-1800 light freighter that had delivered the troopers to the depot, where Chatterbox had been shot in the back by a battle droid. Knuckles and Breaker had removed Chatterbox's armor so they could apply coagulants and flesh-healing bacta patches to his wounded torso. Breaker had set up the intravenous transfusion kit from an emergency med kit, and both he and Knuckles wore matching bandages across the crooks of their left arms from where they had drawn blood for Chatterbox.

The troopers' commander, the young Jedi Nuru Kungurama, knelt beside Chatterbox. Studying the flow regulator on the transfusion set, Nuru said, "How much blood did you two give?"

"A half liter each," Breaker said.

"He'll need more, and soon."

Knuckles looked around. "Where's Sharp?"

"He said he heard something moving in the adjoining docking bay," Nuru said as he pointed to a nearby doorway. "He wanted to make sure it wasn't another battle droid."

Knuckles picked up a comlink and said, "Sharp? Do you read me? Chatterbox needs your blood."

A burst of static came from the comlink, and then Sharp's voice replied, "I . . . I read you. Are you sure it's my turn?"

"Your *turn?*" Knuckles said impatiently. "You haven't given any yet! Get back to the docking bay now!"

Chatterbox groaned in pain. Knuckles set aside the comlink and returned his attention to his wounded ally.

"Hey, kid!" a deep voice roared from the nearby freighter. Breaker and Nuru turned to see Gizz, a giant, orange-skinned humanoid and swoop biker whom Nuru had befriended on the planet Vaced. Poking his large head out through the open hatch above the freighter's boarding ramp, Gizz said, "I found something you gotta see!"

Nuru was about to respond when he saw Sharp, fully clad in white armor, step through a doorway on the far side of the docking bay. Knuckles saw Sharp, too, and said, "Move it, Sharp!"

Nuru watched Sharp take a cautious step forward. Sharp held his blaster rifle so its barrel was aimed at the floor in front of him, but Nuru noticed he had one finger on his rifle's trigger.

"What's wrong with you?" Knuckles said. "Get over here!"

Nuru sensed something was indeed wrong with Sharp, something . . . *dangerous*? Ever since Sharp had told Nuru that he suspected a saboteur might be traveling with Breakout Squad, the Jedi had noticed that Sharp seemed anxious and mistrustful. Rising from Chatterbox's side, Nuru positioned himself between Sharp and the other troopers. Two lightsabers were clipped to Nuru's belt, and he held his hand ready to draw and activate one if Sharp opened fire.

Sharp removed his finger from his rifle's trigger, lowered his weapon, and moved one hand to touch the armor that covered his stomach. "I don't feel well. I think I'm . . . I'm sick."

"Sick?" Knuckles said. "What in blazes do you—?"

"Listen," Breaker interrupted as he looked to the docking bay's wide entrance. "Here comes the cruiser!"

While the other members of Breakout Squad watched the one-hundred-and-fifteen-meter-long *Consular*-class Republic Cruiser ease its heavily armored nose into the docking bay, Nuru Kungurama kept his red eyes fixed on Sharp. The danger that Nuru thought he had sensed from Sharp seemed to have completely vanished. A moment later, the cruiser's landing jets fired, kicking up dust across the deck.

"Hey, kid!" Gizz repeated. "You really gotta see what I—"

"Not now, Gizz," Nuru said. "We're busy out here."

Gizz grumbled as he ducked back into the freighter. As the cruiser settled onto the deck, Knuckles said, "Commander, should we say anything about Aristocra and Ring-Sol Ambase?"

Nuru's mind reeled. Less than an hour earlier, he and Breakout Squad had had a very unexpected meeting with Aristocra Sev'eere'nuruodo, also known as Veeren, the Chiss ambassador he had met previously on a mission to Chiss space. Veeren had used a tracking device to follow Nuru to Bilbringi Depot and had told him she believed an unknown enemy was conspiring to conquer the galaxy. She claimed the conspiracy dated back at least eleven years and possibly coincided with the Jedi discovering the Chiss escape pod that carried Nuru as an infant. She had forbidden Nuru from telling the Jedi Council about her suspicions because she also believed spies and assassins could be anywhere, and that Nuru's life as well as her own were in danger. Unfortunately, as Veeren was leaving Bilbringi Depot in her starship, another ship, a Kuat *Corona*-class transport, arrived. Veeren's ship fired lasers at the *Corona*, and the *Corona* returned fire. Veeren's ship exploded.

Like all Jedi, Nuru had been trained to live without emotional attachments or anger, and to remain calm when he used the power of the Force, but he had felt almost overwhelmed by the grief and rage that struck him when he saw Veeren's ship destroyed. And through the Force, he'd sensed that the *Corona* was helmed by his own Jedi Master, Ring-Sol Ambase.

Nuru's only evidence of his meeting with Veeren was the Chiss tracking device, a small, gray cylinder with a magnetic strip on the side that he'd since secured to his belt. As he removed the device from his belt and tucked it into a pocket, he looked at Breaker. "Say nothing about Veeren or Ambase."

"But, Commander, maybe you *should* tell the Jedi Council about Aristocra. I mean, if everything she said is true—"

"Then we have every reason *not* to tell the Council. Not a word about what happened, and that's an order."

"Yes, sir," Breaker replied, but Nuru could tell that Breaker questioned the order.

The members of Breakout Squad were not the only ones aware of the Republic Cruiser's arrival at Bilbringi Depot. Nearly twenty-one kilometers away from the asteroidal station, the silver-haired Jedi Master Ring-Sol Ambase sat in a needle-nosed, ridged-back Kuat *Corona*-class transport. The transport rested in the shadows of a cluster of asteroids, and Ambase had switched off all the transport's electronic systems and sensors to prevent other vessels from detecting the transport's location. He peered through a pair of macrobinoculars that he'd found in a supply box and searched for signs of any other Republic vessels.

Ambase's companion in the *Corona* was a clone trooper named Sharp, who, like Ambase, was unaware of the fact that another trooper, also named Sharp, was in the company of Breakout Squad.

Sharp was trying to repair the transport's communications systems, which had been damaged when he and Ambase fled Count Dooku's castle during an aerial bombardment. Looking away from a tangle of wires, Sharp said, "General, I don't think it's safe for you to remain in the Bilbringi system."

"I want to know what Nuru is up to," Ambase said. "And if we leave now, the Republic Cruiser's sensors will spot us."

"But there may be more Jedi on that cruiser. If what Dooku said is true, then—"

"Then the Sith Lords are manipulating the Jedi and the Senate, and also turning apprentices against their own Masters. But that's according to Dooku, and I'm not convinced he was telling the truth. For all we know, Dooku is a Sith Lord."

"But, General, he wasn't lying about Nuru Kungurama seizing Bilbringi Depot. And when that strange spacecraft fired at us from the depot, your Padawan did nothing to stop it."

"So it seems," Ambase said as he lowered the macrobinoculars. "But that spacecraft was similar in design to the escape pod that was carrying Nuru when Dooku and I discovered the boy. I wonder if the spacecraft was another Chiss vessel."

"Would that be bad?"

"Perhaps. The Jedi know little about the Chiss. Nuru's escape pod contained data and technology we could barely understand." Ambase glanced at Sharp and said, "Speaking of technology, are you sure you can get the comm to work again?"

"I think so. I'm more concerned about the rest of the transport. We took quite a beating when we escaped Dooku's castle." Recalling how they'd seen the wreckage of Dooku's solar sailer before they'd fled in the Corona, Sharp said, "I wish we could have confirmed whether Dooku is still alive."

"Add that to a number of things I'd like to confirm," Ambase said. He looked through the macrobinoculars and returned his attention to Bilbringi Depot.

The Republic cruiser's hatch hissed open and the Jedi Master Kit Fisto stepped down to the docking bay floor. An amphibious Nautolan, Kit Fisto had green skin and long tentacles that extended from his head and dangled down his back. Like many other Jedi Masters, he had become a general in the Republic Army, which had been created to fight the Separatists and their legions of battle droids.

A platoon of clone troopers followed Kit Fisto down the cruiser's boarding ramp, followed by a team of clone medics. Two medics guided a repulsorlift stretcher into the docking bay.

"Hurry up with that stretcher!" Knuckles shouted.

The medics ran over to Knuckles and Breaker, who remained hunkered down beside Chatterbox. "He was shot in the back," Breaker said. "We gave him two units of blood."

Knuckles looked at Sharp, who was walking slowly toward him. Sharp still had one hand placed against the lower half of his chest plate. Knuckles said, "If you're feeling sick, you should let the medics look at you."

Sharp shook his head. "Let them take care of Chatterbox first. I'll be all right."

Nuru watched the medics move Chatterbox onto the stretcher. One medic adjusted the stretcher's elevation controls, raising it to hover a full meter above the ground while another medic picked up Chatterbox's helmet. As the medics brought Chatterbox to the cruiser and the just-arrived platoon fanned out across the docking bay, Nuru turned to see Kit Fisto approaching from the cruiser.

Kit Fisto came to a stop before Nuru. Nuru kept his expression calm as he bowed. "Greetings, Master Fisto."

Fisto bowed in return. "Master Yoda told me where to find you. I came as soon as I could. You're a long way from home, young one. But from what I've heard, you've also been very busy."

Nuru wondered how much Fisto knew about his actions over the past few weeks. His red eyes flicked to the Republic cruiser. "I'm concerned about Chatterbox . . . the wounded trooper."

"The medics will do everything they can," Kit Fisto said.

"Of course," Nuru said solemnly. "Did Master Yoda relay my report about what happened on Vaced?"

"He said your mission did not go as planned, but that you came to Bilbringi Depot and managed to capture Overseer Umbrag. He said you would give me details."

Nuru had almost forgotten about the Skakoan Overseer Umbrag of the Techno Union, who was allied with the Separatists. Nuru shook his head. "Forgive me, Master. I'm not sure where to begin."

"I'm aware that you left the Jedi Temple to follow Ring-Sol Ambase to Kynachi, and how you led a group of clone troopers to liberate Kynachi from Overseer Umbrag's Separatist occupation. I also know that Ambase went missing on Kynachi, and that Master Yoda reluctantly authorized you to command your improvised unit, Breakout Squad, on two covert missions." Fisto looked at the three clone troopers who stood at attention nearby and added, "Breakout Squad?"

Nuru said. "Master Fisto, meet Breaker, Knuckles, and Sharp."

Fisto nodded at the troopers. "I commend you for your actions at Kynachi."

Breaker said, "Thank you, General."

Fisto looked at Nuru. "What happened on Vaced, and what brought you to Bilbringi?"

Choosing his words carefully, Nuru replied, "Breakout Squad and I were returning to Coruscant in a freighter owned by Lalo Gunn, a pilot we met on Kynachi, when we received a transmission from Master Yoda and Chancellor Palpatine. They instructed us to change course for Vaced so we could rendezvous with Commissioner Langu Sommilor, a representative from Kynachi, and escort him to Coruscant for a special meeting with the Senate. The chancellor said Republic Intelligence had reason to believe the Techno Union might try to stop the commissioner from reaching Coruscant. We took precautions, but just after the commissioner's freighter landed, an assassin killed Sommilor and his two pilots. The assassin wore Mandalorian armor."

"But the Mandalorians ended their warrior ways years ago," Fisto said. "Theirs is a peaceful world. Perhaps the assassin was an imposter?"

"All I know is he was an expert sniper and martial artist. He might have killed me if a swoop biker named Gizz hadn't joined the fight. Lalo Gunn blasted the assassin's ship out of the sky over Vaced."

"You're certain the assassin is dead?"

"We saw his ship explode. He couldn't have survived. However, Cleaver found—"

"Who is Cleaver?"

"Forgive me, Master. Cleaver is a droid commando that we refurbished with parts from Lalo Gunn's former droid copilot. Cleaver is very loyal and works with us. On Vaced, he found a utility belt. We suspected the assassin either dropped the belt or deliberately left it behind. One of the belt's pouches held an imagecaster, and the only thing on it was a map of the Bilbringi system. I wanted to investigate, and we left Vaced in Commissioner Sommilor's ship." Nuru pointed to the thirty-meter-long Suwantek Systems freighter.

The clone troopers of Breakout Squad noticed that Nuru had not mentioned the fact that the utility belt Cleaver had found belonged to Ring-Sol Ambase. Apparently, Kit Fisto was not curious about the belt or its origin, for he looked at the Suwantek freighter and said, "You're no longer traveling with Lalo Gunn?"

"Her ship was destroyed during the fight with the assassin," Nuru said. "She decided to part ways with us on Vaced, which surprised me."

"Why?"

"Because she seemed fond of Chatterbox."

Fisto looked at Nuru and said, "Fond?"

"Yes. Very fond."

"Oh." Looking back at the Suwantek freighter, Fisto said, "You brought the bodies of Sommilor and the pilots with you?"

"Yes, Master. I anticipated someone would send the bodies back to Kynachi."

"Before you left Vaced, why didn't you send a transmission to Coruscant to alert the Jedi Temple about what had happened or where you were going?"

"We learned there was a tracking device on Lalo Gunn's ship. I didn't know whether the assassin or someone else had planted the device, but I allowed the possibility that someone was still monitoring Breakout Squad's movements and communications. I chose not to send any transmission that might have been intercepted by an enemy."

"That's practical of you. So you arrived here and found Overseer Umbrag?"

Nuru nodded. "His yacht and six drone barges are in the adjoining docking bay. It seems Umbrag and a small number of battle droids had seized the depot, but they weren't prepared for us."

"According to my data, Bilbringi Depot is owned by a Hutt named Drixo. Any sign of Drixo or her servants?"

"No, Master."

"Did you inspect the drone barges?"

"Yes. We only checked to make sure there weren't any droids on board, but the barges appear to be filled to capacity with construction materials and building supplies."

"Do you know what Umbrag was planning on building?"

"No, Master."

"Where is Umbrag now?"

Nuru pointed to the Suwantek freighter again. "Gizz and Cleaver are guarding him."

"Gizz?" Fisto said with surprise. "The swoop biker you mentioned? He came here, too?"

"If we'd left him on Vaced, his circumstances might have become . . . unfortunately complicated. I felt obligated to help him. Anyway, after we captured Umbrag, I sent a transmission to the Jedi Council. But then one last remaining battle droid took us by surprise and shot Chatterbox." Nuru looked at Breaker and said, "I believe that's all there is to tell."

"Not quite," Fisto said. "I see you're carrying your Master's lightsaber as well as your own. How did you come by that?"

Nuru brushed his fingers against the two lightsabers at his belt. "On Kynachi, we met a bounty hunter who claimed he found Master Ambase's lightsaber. He gave it to me. I . . . I'd hoped to return it to my Master."

Fisto placed a hand on Nuru's shoulder. "You, too, are to be commended for your actions, young one. But now, it's time for you to return to Coruscant while my team secures this facility and—"

Fisto was distracted by the sudden noise of his entire platoon switching off the safety controls on their blaster rifles. Nuru saw that Fisto's platoon had trained their weapons at the Suwantek freighter's hatch, where a skeletal droid with glowing eyes had just emerged.

"Hold fire and lower your weapons!" Nuru said as Breaker and Knuckles jumped in front of the nearest members of Fisto's platoon, blocking them from firing at Cleaver. "The droid commando is completely reprogrammed and won't hurt you. He's with Breakout Squad."

The troopers looked to Kit Fisto. Fisto nodded once, and the troopers lowered their rifles. Knuckles said, "That was a close one, Cleaver. We'll have to be more careful with you around troopers in the future."

"That would be a relief to all," Cleaver said as he stepped down the freighter's boarding ramp.

Nuru glanced at Fisto and whispered, "Cleaver hopes to become a Jedi."

Fisto grinned. "Well, doesn't everyone?"

Cleaver came to a stop before the two Jedi. Nuru said, "Cleaver, allow me to introduce you to Jedi General Fisto."

Cleaver bowed and said, "It is my honor, General." He turned to Nuru. "Commander

Kungurama, you should know that Gizz discovered three men hidden in the freighter."

"Something must be wrong with your memory, Cleaver. Before we left Vaced, you helped bag and move the bodies of Commissioner Sommilor and his two pilots into a storage compartment. Don't you remember?"

"But I'm not talking about the dead men, Commander. Gizz found three men who are *alive*. They were in a different storage compartment."

"Are they . . . stowaways?"

"Not precisely. They were bound and gagged. It appears they were captives."

Fisto looked at Nuru and said, "You do travel with unusual company."

"What's most odd," Cleaver continued, "is that they claim to be Commissioner Sommilor and the pilots from Kynachi."

Nuru's red eyes went wide with surprise. Fisto said, "I'd like to have a word with these men."

"So would I," Nuru said as he headed for the freighter.

CHAPTER 3

Breaker, Knuckles, Sharp, and Cleaver followed Nuru Kungurama and Kit Fisto into the freighter. They found Gizz in the main cabin, his back hunched so he wouldn't hit his broad head against the ceiling as he handed mugs filled with water to three men who were seated on an acceleration bench. One man wore a blue uniform, and the other two wore green tunics that were adorned with triangular orange insignias, identifying them as KynachTech pilots. All three had gold hair that was a typical characteristic of people from Kynachi. Looking at Nuru, Gizz said, "What took you so long?"

"Gizz, meet General Fisto."

"Another Jedi, huh?" Gizz said as he raised his thick fingers of his right hand in a casual salute.

Fisto bowed slightly to Gizz, and Nuru noticed Fisto's nostrils close in a reflexive response to Gizz's body odor. Stepping back from Gizz, Fisto faced the three seated men and said, "Are you all right?"

The men nodded. Gizz said, "They're still a little groggy. I think they were knocked out by something."

Knuckles leaned close to Breaker and whispered, "It's a wonder they're not knocked out by the smell of Gizz."

Gizz's tapered ears twitched, and he growled, "I heard that, Knucklehead."

The man in the blue uniform took a long drink of water, cleared his throat, and said, "I'm Commissioner Sommilor from Kynachi." Gesturing to the two men seated with him, he added, "My pilots, Pikkson and Sunmantle." He shifted his gaze to the young, blue-skinned Jedi and said, "You . . . you're Nuru Kungurama. I saw you on Kynachi. The people of my world are in your debt for saving us from the Techno Union."

Neither Fisto nor Nuru sensed that the man was lying, but they also knew they needed more information before they could decide whether he was trustworthy. Removing a small scanner device from his utility belt, Fisto said, "May we transmit a data scan to the Kynachi authorities to confirm your identity?"

"Of course."

Fisto aimed the scanner at the seated men, then plugged the device into the main hold's comm console. "It will take a few minutes to get a response from Kynachi."

Facing the man who claimed to be Sommilor, Nuru said, "Do you recall Chancellor Palpatine introducing us via a hypercomm conference, directing me to meet you on Vaced and escort you to Coruscant?"

"Vaced?" The man shook his head. "No. No, that couldn't have been me. You and the chancellor must have been talking with the imposter."

"Imposter?"

The man in the blue uniform nodded. Gesturing to the pilots beside him, he said, "We were on Kynachi, preparing to leave for Coruscant. I was to meet with Republic Senators about an alliance. The people of Kynachi want to join your fight against the Separatists." He took another sip of water. "We were still on the launch pad when three men attacked us. They put on masks, disguised themselves to look like us. They made us swallow doze tablets before they put us in binders and locked us in the aft hold."

Nuru turned to Breaker and whispered, "Inspect the three bodies that we brought from Vaced. See if they're wearing disguises."

As Breaker exited the main hold, Fisto faced the man in the blue uniform and said, "Did you recognize the men who captured you?"

"No. They were strangers, not from Kynachi. Maybe they were mercenaries. Did . . . did you apprehend them?"

"Before I answer that, can you tell me whether you have any enemies? Anyone who might have hired mercenaries to abduct and impersonate you?"

The man thought for a moment, then said, "The only person I can think of is Overseer Umbrag. He must be furious about how the Republic troopers drove his forces off Kynachi. Or . . . of course! The Techno Union must have wanted to stop me from reaching Coruscant!"

Gizz aimed a thick thumb at a sealed hatch and said, "We got Umbrag locked up tight in there. He could tell us."

Nuru said, "But what if he refuses to talk?"

"Then I'll make him talk." Before anyone could intervene, Gizz opened the hatch and squeezed his bulk into the next chamber. Inside, he found Umbrag sitting on a bench, huddled against a metal bulkhead. The Skakoan was wearing thick-lensed goggles and a protective armored pressure suit. The only parts of his body that was exposed and unprotected were the top and back of his green-skinned head. Metal gauntlets covered his wrists, which were secured by binder cuffs. A second set of binders was clamped around his ankles.

Umbrag looked up at Gizz and said meekly, "If I am a prisoner of war, I have certain rights!"

"Shut up, ugly," Gizz said as he sealed the hatch behind him.

From the other side of the hatch, Umbrag and Gizz heard Nuru's muffled voice shout, "Gizz, what are you doing?"

Ignoring Nuru, Gizz stared hard at Umbrag and said, "See this?" He held up his massive right hand

and made a fist that was almost as large as Umbrag's head. "This here hand of mine is what I call the lie detector. You lie to me, and the hand gets angry. Then the hand starts pounding whatever's within reach, and there's absolutely nothing I can do to stop it. Nothing personal, Umbrag, that's just how it works. Understand?"

Umbrag let out a horrified squeaking sound as he nodded.

"Good. What I wanna know is . . . do you know a guy named Sommilor from Kynachi?"

Umbrag looked surprised. "Sommilor? I . . . I think he was a local politician of some kind."

Gizz flexed the fingers of his right hand, making the knuckles pop loudly before making a fist again. "Did you try to stop him from going to Coruscant?"

"You mean . . . during the occupation of Kynachi?"

"I mean," Gizz said through clenched teeth as he leaned closer to Umbrag, "did you hire goons to stop him from going to Coruscant?"

"No!" Umbrag shrieked. "No! I don't know what you're talking about!"

Gizz bared his sharp teeth and snarled, "You're lying."

"No!" Umbrag repeated as he raised his manacled wrists to protect his head. "I swear I didn't hire anyone to stop Sommilor!"

Gizz grinned. "Okay," he said as he turned, opened the hatch, and squeezed through it to rejoin Nuru and the others. As he sealed the hatch, he looked at Nuru and Fisto and said, "Umbrag doesn't know nothin'."

"Thank you for your assistance, Mister Gizz," Fisto said, "but the Jedi prefer less violent methods of interrogation."

Gizz shrugged, and his shoulders made a thudding noise as they struck the ceiling. "Suit yourselves."

Breaker returned to the main hold. "It's true about the disguises, Commander," he said. "The dead men are wearing synthskin masks and gold wigs."

The man in the blue uniform raised his eyebrows and said, "Dead men?"

Gizz said, "Synthskin?"

A loud beep sounded from the comm console. Kit Fisto removed his scanner, studied its tiny datascreen, then said, "KynachTech has confirmed your identity, Commissioner Sommilor. Nuru, tell the commissioner and pilots what happened on the planet Vaced."

Nuru said, "The men who impersonated you were killed by a sniper. The sniper tried to kill us, too, but he died when his ship exploded. We don't know whether he was operating alone or following orders."

Sommilor shuddered, then said, "But . . . was the sniper trying to kill me and my pilots, or did he know he was shooting at imposters? And if the imposters were trying to stop me from reaching Coruscant, why didn't they just kill me on Kynachi? Why the charade?"

"Those are very good questions," Fisto said. "If we can identify the imposters, we might find an answer."

Gizz said, "I wanna take a look at those dead guys." He ambled across the main hold and ducked through the hatch that led to the compartment that contained the bodies.

Fisto looked at Knuckles and said, "Go with him. Make sure he doesn't tamper with any evidence." As

Knuckles followed Gizz out of the main hold, Fisto turned back to face Sommilor and said, "For all we know, you may still be targeted for assassination. Do you wish to proceed to Coruscant, or would you rather return to Kynachi? Either way, you shall have a military escort."

Before Sommilor could answer, the pilot named Pikkson gasped as Gizz walked back into the main hold with a dead man slung over his shoulder. The corpse was the man who had impersonated Sommilor. Gizz was followed by Knuckles, who caught Fisto's glare and said, "I'm sorry, General. He just grabbed the body. I couldn't stop him."

Fisto said, "Mister Gizz, what's the meaning of this—?"

"No need for mister. Just call me Gizz," Gizz said as he lowered the corpse onto a table near the seated men. "I should've thought of this when Breaker mentioned the synthskin masks, but it was all that babble about who knows what or doesn't know whatever that really got me thinking. Only one gang I ever heard of does everything *that* sneaky and confusing."

Nuru said, "Gizz, you're not making any sense. What gang?"

Gizz pushed up the sleeve on the dead man's right arm to reveal a smooth area of flesh. "See there? That's synthskin, right?"

"It appears to be," Fisto said as he moved closer to the corpse.

"Let's see what it's covering." Gizz pinched the smooth flesh and yanked it away, revealing a black, circular tattoo on the man's forearm. The tattoo had an outer ring of pointed spines.

Kit Fisto's eyes widened at the sight of the tattoo. "Black Sun."

"Yep," Gizz said. "I guessed right." He looked at Nuru. "I don't even want to try to imagine what these guys had planned for you, kid. If you ask me, the sniper did us all a favor." He tossed the synthskin over his shoulder, and it hit Sharp's armor with a wet, slapping sound.

"I . . . I think I'm going to be ill," Sharp said.

"Go see the medics, Sharp," Nuru said. "You can check on Chatterbox for us while you're at it."

As Sharp shuffled out of the freighter, Knuckles muttered, "Sharp's really not himself lately."

Sommilor said, "General Fisto, can you tell me . . . what is Black Sun?"

"A criminal organization. Very secretive, and very powerful."

"Do you think the Separatists hired Black Sun to kidnap me?"

Fisto shook his head slightly, making his tentacles jiggle. "I'm not sure what to think. If the Separatists hired Black Sun, then who hired the sniper? And was the sniper really a Mandalorian or just a rogue in Mandalorian armor? All we know for certain is that we're dealing with deadly adversaries. So tell us, Commissioner . . . how do *you* want to proceed?"

Sommilor looked at Pikkson and Sunmantle, then said, "This experience has been most distressing, but it has also made me even *more* resolved to secure an alliance with the Republic. I don't know why the Separatists took such extraordinary measures to prevent me from reaching my meeting with the Senate, but they *must* be behind all this skulduggery, and I won't allow them to scare me off. I wish to proceed to Coruscant."

Fisto bowed. "As you wish. But first, I must secure Bilbringi Depot."

Knuckles said, "Excuse me, General, but . . . even though Chancellor Palpatine and General Yoda were unaware that they were dealing with imposters from Kynachi, they *did* entrust Nuru Kungurama and Breakout Squad to escort the commissioner to his meeting. Unless anyone objects, I for one would like to finish that assignment."

Fisto looked from Nuru to Sommilor and said, "Any objections?"

Nuru said, "Commissioner Sommilor, I was unprepared for what happened on Vaced. I will understand if you would prefer to travel with a senior Jedi."

Sommilor smiled. "I don't think *anyone* could have been prepared for what happened on Vaced. But without you and Breakout Squad, the Techno Union might still be occupying my world. I would be honored if you escorted me to Coruscant."

Fisto smiled. "So be it. And Breakout Squad can also deliver Overseer Umbrag to the Republic authorities for further questioning."

Nuru said, "Master Fisto, do you know whether reports of Commissioner Sommilor's death have reached the Galactic Senate?"

"I'm not certain, but news does travel fast these days."

"Then I request that you don't notify anyone that the Commissioner and his men are still alive, that we allow others to believe they died on Vaced. That way, we have a better chance of delivering them safely to the Senate because, well . . . assassins don't try to kill dead men."

"A wise move." Fisto began to turn away, then he stopped and said, "Oh! I forgot to tell you earlier, Nuru . . . when you arrive at Coruscant, you should contact the Jedi scholar Harro Kelpura in the Jedi Archives. He wants to talk with you about the escape pod in which Master Ambase found you. He said he'd deciphered some significant data."

Wondering if the data were related to his heritage, Nuru said, "Did he mention what type of data?"

Fisto shook his tentacled head. "You'll have to ask Kelpura."

The trooper that Breakout Squad thought was Sharp wore his helmet as he left the Suwantek freighter. He did not go straight to the clone medics who were with Chatterbox in the Republic cruiser. Instead, he walked across the docking bay, passing members of Kit Fisto's platoon, and went through a hatch that led to a shadowy corridor where he knew he would have at least a few minutes of privacy.

The holocomm unit that he removed from his utility belt appeared to be a standard military-issue device, but it had been modified for long-range encrypted transmissions across space. As he held the holocomm in one hand and tapped the small data keys with his thumb, he used his other hand to remove his helmet, revealing the strong features of a clone soldier.

He glanced up and down the corridor to make sure no one was approaching and then exhaled. The color of his flesh shifted to a grayish green. He blinked his eyes, and they changed from brown to yellow, from human to reptilian—revealing his true form as a shape-shifting Clawdite.

The holocomm projected a flickering light that transformed into a hologram, a three-dimensional image of a woman's head. She was bald with ghastly white skin and pale blue eyes. The Clawdite had no difficulty recognizing the assassin Asajj Ventress.

Ventress said, "You should have reported to me hours ago."

"I don't have much time," said the Clawdite. "Things went wrong on Vaced. Lalo Gunn's ship crashed. A Mandalorian assassin and Black Sun were involved."

"What?!"

"Now I'm with Breakout Squad at Bilbringi Depot."

Bilbringi?! Ventress suddenly recalled her recent meeting with the Duros bounty hunter on the moon Bogg 5. The bounty hunter had delivered two stasis pods that contained the unconscious forms of the Jedi Ring-Sol Ambase and a single clone trooper.

Dooku had instructed her to send the Duros bounty hunter to Bilbringi, and she knew Breakout Squad's arrival to Bilbringi could not be a coincidence. She said, "Why did you go to Bilbringi?"

"We . . . I mean *they've* captured Overseer Umbrag," the Clawdite said breathlessly. "A Republic cruiser just arrived with a platoon of troopers, and . . ." Glancing back up the corridor to make sure he was still alone, he continued, "You have to get me out of here. Breakout Squad almost made me give blood for a wounded clone. I pretended I was sick, but they must be getting suspicious. It's only a matter of time before—"

"Enough!" Ventress snapped. "Stay with Breakout Squad. I will contact you in one hour with new orders."

"New orders? But . . . but I've already done everything you asked!"

"And you'll *keep doing* what I tell you, shapeshifter, or our deal is off."

"Wait! I don't even know where I'll be in one hour. You can't expect me to—"

The hologram flickered and died. The Clawdite stared at the empty air for a moment, then returned the holocomm to his belt and put his helmet back on. As he walked back to the docking bay and headed for the Republic cruiser, he tried to control his breathing and remain calm.

The clone troopers who were stationed outside the cruiser did not take any special notice of the armored Clawdite as he approached. The Clawdite said, "I'm Sharp, with Breakout Squad. I'd like to check in with the medics to see how my friend Chatterbox is doing. Permission to come aboard?"

"Permission granted, and we hope your brother pulls through."

"Thanks." The Clawdite stepped up into the cruiser and moved down a narrow corridor until he reached the infirmary, where a trooper directed him to a trauma room. The Clawdite looked through a window to see a team of clone medics and a multilimbed medical assistant droid operating on Chatterbox, who was lying on a med pad. A transparent breath mask covered Chatterbox's nose and mouth, and his eyes were closed.

One of the medics noticed the trooper standing on the other side of the window. The medic stepped out of the room, gave a quick study of the trooper's armor, then extended his right hand and said, "I'm Quills. You're with Breakout Squad?"

The Clawdite shook the medic's hand. "Sharp."

"Glad to know you, Sharp. No need to wear your helmet in here."

The Clawdite winced as he rapidly adjusted his facial muscles and pigmentation to transform his features. When he removed his helmet, his head was almost identical to the medic's. He gestured to the window and said, "How's my friend?"

"We've got him stabilized. Chatterbox is a tough one, he is. If I were a betting man, I'd wager he'll live. I'd like to get him into a recovery facility on Coruscant as soon as possible. When we get back, we'll put him in our best place."

"Well, I . . . I'd better go tell my squad." The Clawdite turned and went to the infirmary's exit, taking his helmet with him, and returned to the docking bay floor.

"Hey, Sharp!" Breaker called out.

The Clawdite jumped slightly as he turned to see Breaker and Nuru Kungurama approaching. Nuru said, "You saw the medics?"

The Clawdite nodded. "Chatterbox is stabilized, but he's unconscious. A medic named Quills said he'll live, but . . . he doesn't look good."

Breaker lifted his gaze to the docking bay's ceiling. Then he closed his eyes, lowered his head, and muttered, "This awful war."

"We'll hope for the best," Nuru said. "How are *you* feeling, Sharp?"

"I'm fine, Commander," the Clawdite said. "I don't know why I got queasy earlier, but it passed."

"You look pale."

"I'm fine. Really fine."

"Good," Nuru said. "We have new orders. We're taking Commissioner Sommilor, his pilots, and Overseer Umbrag in the Suwantek freighter to Coruscant while General Fisto's team finishes securing the depot."

The Clawdite said, "I hope General Fisto won't take long. Quills said Chatterbox should go to a recovery facility on Coruscant as soon as possible."

Breaker said, "Well, if Chatterbox is stabilized, maybe Quills could return with us?"

Nuru said, "I'll check with Quills and General Fisto. I'm sure we all want what's best for Chatterbox."

"Indeed, sir," said the Clawdite.

Quills helped Breaker and Cleaver transfer Chatterbox and the necessary medical equipment from the Republic cruiser to the Suwantek freighter and placed Chatterbox in the freighter's passenger quarters. Quills also confirmed that the Kynachi pilots Pikkson and Sunmantle were fit for duty. While the pilots went to the cockpit and Breakout Squad prepared for liftoff, Gizz stayed posted outside the chamber that held Overseer Umbrag.

Minutes later, when the freighter lifted off and moved out of the docking bay, it carried one young Jedi, two active clone troopers, one unconscious clone trooper, one clone medic, one reprogrammed droid commando, one malodorous humanoid giant, one diplomat, two pilots from Kynachi, one Skakoan prisoner, three dead men who bore Black Sun tattoos, and one increasingly anxious Clawdite shape-shifter disguised as a clone trooper.

But by the time the freighter reached Coruscant, the men with the Black Sun tattoos would not be the only dead passengers.

CHAPTER 4

Still hiding in the asteroid belt in the Bilbringi system, Ring-Sol Ambase and the actual clone trooper named Sharp sat inside the *Corona*-class transport and watched the departing Suwantek freighter's thrusters grow bright. Ambase leaned forward in his seat as the freighter transformed into a streak of light that almost immediately vanished in the distance.

Ambase slumped back from the cockpit's window. "Nuru Kungurama was on that freighter."

Sharp cocked his head and said, "Judging from the trajectory of their jump, they're taking the Namadii Corridor, the course that leads to Palanhi."

"And Coruscant."

Sharp looked at Ambase and said, "Do you want to wait for the Republic cruiser to leave the depot before we proceed?"

Ambase was still pondering that question when a burst of static sounded unexpectedly from the comm console. Ambase glanced at Sharp and said, "It's working?"

Sharp examined a datascreen and said, "Yes, General. And we're picking up an encrypted holocomm transmission. It's coming from . . . the Bogden system."

Dooku? Ambase leaned over beside Sharp to face the comm console and said, "The Republic cruiser won't detect the transmission?"

"No, sir. They'll only read static."

"Then let's see it."

Sharp pressed a control button, and a hologram of Dooku materialized over the console. Dooku said, "Ring-Sol! Are you all right?"

Ambase considered whether to respond, then said, "I'm doing better."

"When I realized you and the trooper were missing during the attack on my retreat, I feared the worst. But then I learned a freighter had left my landing pad, and I've been trying to locate you ever since. I'm relieved to know you survived."

Sharp muttered, "I'll bet he is."

Ambase discreetly raised one finger to signal Sharp to remain silent. Keeping his eyes on Dooku's hologram, he said, "We didn't know what happened to you, either. How did you find us?"

"There's a tracking device on the freighter," Dooku said. "After all, the ship *was* my property. Now, I must say, I didn't expect you'd travel to the Bilbringi system. Did you go there just to find out whether I was telling the truth about Nuru Kungurama taking over the depot?"

"Why else?" Ambase said tersely.

"What did you learn?"

Ambase stared hard at the hologram.

"I see," Dooku said. "You found out I was right. I'm sorry your Padawan has taken the dark path. But it's best that you know the truth, that you're prepared, especially after the news from Coruscant."

Ambase stiffened. "What news?"

"A Jedi scholar, Harro Kelpura, has been studying an unusual spacecraft and claims he has successfully deciphered extensive data about the civilization that produced the craft. Most of the data is related to military offensive and defensive systems."

"And you're relaying this information because . . . ?"

"Because the spacecraft is the escape pod that we found in the Unknown Regions eleven years ago."

Looking skeptical, Ambase said, "You expect me to believe you have classified information from the Jedi Archives?"

Dooku shook his head. "No, Ring-Sol. I don't expect you to believe anything I say. If finding Nuru Kungurama on Bilbringi didn't convince you of my sincerity, nothing I say ever will. However, you might be interested in the fact that Harro Kelpura has moved the escape pod from the Archives to an abandoned manufacturing facility at Coruscant's Dacho District for testing purposes. Furthermore, I've learned that someone intends to steal the pod."

Ambase knew the Jedi scholar Harro Kelpura well and struggled to maintain an impassive expression as he eyed Dooku's hologram. He said, "I won't bother questioning whether you're telling the truth. But I do question your motives for telling me anything at all."

"Why?"

"Because if anyone were scheming to steal an alien vessel containing data that might be used against enemies, my first suspect would be the leader of the Confederacy. Hence, I wonder why you'd warn any Jedi in advance."

Dooku sighed. "I didn't notify just any Jedi, old friend. I contacted you."

Surprised, Ambase said, "You mean . . . you *don't* want the pod for the Confederacy?"

"Of course not."

"Then what *do* you want?"

"When you and I discovered the Chiss escape pod, I said that it might be used as a key to another realm of space. While some might try to use such a key in good faith and with noble ambitions, the fact is that some alien civilizations are not eager to meet outsiders. Sometimes, a key can unlock the unexpected, and afterward, it's too late to lock things up again."

"You believe the Chiss are a threat?"

"Ring-Sol, the key itself is a threat. We know practically nothing about the Chiss. Therefore, we must allow the possibility that their military strength is greater than the Republic and the Confederacy combined. Can you imagine how using the escape pod's data might cause a confrontation with the Chiss? A confrontation that not only escalates war across the galaxy, but far beyond the Outer Rim? I can imagine that possibility, and I won't have that blood on my hands. It would be best for all if the pod were sent straight into Coruscant's sun."

Ambase shook his head. "I still don't know why you're telling *me* all this."

"Because you and I found the pod and brought it to Coruscant. Although we were only briefly its guardians, we remain responsible for our actions. Now, the key to Chiss space is about to fall into the hands of an opportunist. We can't let that happen."

"Do you know who's planning to steal it?"

"Yes," Dooku said. "Nuru Kungurama."

"Nuru?!"

"A reliable informant told me Nuru has already established contact with the Chiss, that he recently met with a Chiss ambassador at Bilbringi Depot. I wouldn't be surprised if he has formed an alliance with the Chiss, an alliance that will serve the Sith Lords."

Ambase thought of the rage he had sensed from Nuru when the unidentified starship exploded as it was leaving Bilbringi Depot and wondered again if the ship had been a Chiss vessel. He looked at Sharp and could tell from the clone trooper's grim expression that he didn't trust Dooku.

Sharp said, "It's your call, General."

Ambase returned his gaze to Dooku's hologram and said quickly, "The abandoned facility where Harro Kelpura moved the escape pod . . . where is it?"

Hearing the urgency in the Jedi's voice, Dooku had no doubt that Ambase would soon be heading for Coruscant.

Asajj Ventress scowled as she steered her Fanblade starfighter down through the rainy atmosphere of Kohlma, a moon in the Bogden system. She was not looking forward to her meeting with Count Dooku.

She brought her Fanblade down on the landing pad beside Dooku's castle, a dark, spired structure that appeared to grow from the upper rim of a high mountain. She could see no evidence of the mock bombardment that had been engineered to encourage Ring-Sol Ambase and the clone trooper named Sharp to leave in a Kuat transport. She climbed out of her starfighter, walked fast toward the castle, and was already drenched when she saw Dooku waiting for her outside the castle's entrance.

A disc-shaped repulsorlift device hovered above Dooku's head and emitted a thin energy shield that prevented the rain from reaching his body. Holding his hands behind his back, Dooku said, "Your report."

"Lalo Gunn's ship crashed on Vaced," Ventress rasped. "The Clawdite went with Breakout Squad to Bilbringi Depot, where they captured Overseer Umbrag. And then a Republic cruiser arrived at Bilbringi with a platoon of clone troopers. I suspect he has gone insane. He was babbling about Mandalorians and Black Sun."

Stepping away from the castle's entrance, Dooku began walking slowly around Ventress. "These developments are most unfortunate. I invested a great deal of time and money into securing Bilbringi

Depot so it could be transformed into a shipyard for the Separatist fleet." Stopping beside Ventress, Dooku added, "You know how I deal with failure."

Ventress spun to face Dooku and snapped, "But *you* told me to hire the Clawdite for this assignment and to send the Duros bounty hunter to Bilbringi. If *they* failed to—"

Dooku silenced Ventress with his penetrating gaze. "I'm not interested in excuses. I want results."

Ventress lowered her head. "I do everything you ask, Master. Everything. But I don't understand why you involved the Clawdite or the Duros. If you had allowed me to capture Nuru Kungurama on Kynachi, I could have—"

"Did you instruct the Clawdite to remain with Breakout Squad?"

"Yes, Master."

"Then leave now," Dooku interrupted. "I will contact you when I have a need for your limited services."

Without another word, Ventress returned to her starfighter. After her fighter lifted off and vanished into the sky, Dooku walked back into his castle. Leaving his personal rain-deflector hovering near the doorway, he proceeded to his communications room and opened a transmission to the Sith Lord Darth Sidious.

A hologram of Darth Sidious's hooded visage materialized in the air above Dooku's comm console. Only the lower half of Sidious's face was visible as his eyes were lost within the shadows of his cowl. Dooku bowed and said, "My Master."

Addressing Dooku by his Sith Lord name, Sidious replied, "Lord Tyranus. You spoke with Ring-Sol Ambase?"

"Yes. He is on his way to Coruscant."

"Excellent. And what of Ventress?"

"She has reported that Breakout Squad captured Overseer Umbrag and seized Bilbringi Depot. When this news reaches the Hutt Cartel, they will no doubt contact the Galactic Senate to dispute the Republic's takeover of Drixo the Hutt's property."

"I shall deal with the Hutts," Sidious said, his mouth twisting into a sneering smile. "I trust Ventress remains ignorant of our schemes."

"Completely. She has no idea that I arranged for Black Sun to capture and impersonate Commissioner Sommilor and his pilots or that I contracted the

Mandalorian Death Watch to assassinate the men from Kynachi. Beyond her anger, I sensed only her confusion. She actually believes I'm disappointed about losing Kynachi and Bilbringi to the Republic."

Sidious's lips twitched, and his smile vanished. "Ventress also believes she may become your apprentice. If you only manipulate her to fail, she will rise against you sooner than later. She will disobey your orders and try to make you fail. Do not allow her to become a liability."

"I will be mindful, my Master." Dooku replied. "Should we be concerned about Overseer Umbrag?"

"Umbrag has outlived his usefulness. Is the Clawdite spy still traveling with Breakout Squad?"

"Yes."

"Has Ventress instruct the Clawdite to dispose of Umbrag?"

"It will be done," Dooku said with a nod. "Ventress mentioned that the Clawdite was 'babbling' about Mandalorians and Black Sun. Although we expected Breakout Squad to eventually identify the Black Sun agents, we did not intend for them to identify the Mandalorian sniper on Vaced. Evidently, they did."

The edges of Sidious's mouth twisted down. "That is unfortunate. It is too early for the Galactic Senate to learn of the existence of the Mandalorian Death Watch. Steps must be taken to make everyone, including Breakout Squad, believe the sniper was *not* a Mandalorian."

"The Death Watch should clean up their own mess. I will contact their leader immediately after I talk with Ventress."

"Do it," Sidious said. "No one must suspect our maneuverings. And if anyone ever does, it will be far, far too late for them to do anything to stop us." Sidious bared his teeth. "Ring-Sol Ambase will soon confront Nuru Kungurama on Coruscant. I can *feel* it. And after they meet, one will be a Jedi no more."

"But which one, my Master?"

Sidious leered. "That would be telling."

Sidious's hologram faded out. Wasting no time, Dooku keyed a transmission directly to Ventress's Fanblade starfighter. A hologram of Ventress's head appeared before Dooku. Ventress said, "My Master."

"Contact the Clawdite. Tell him to kill Overseer Umbrag."

Betraying no surprise at the Dooku's instruction, Ventress replied, "Yes, my Master."

Dooku broke the connection with Ventress, then keyed a transmission to a secret location on Concordia, one of the two moons in orbit of the planet Mandalore. Several seconds later, a hologram of a Mandalorian warrior wearing a dark T-visored helmet appeared before Dooku. The helmet was adorned with a trident symbol above the visor and concealed the head of the Death Watch's leader.

Facing the hologram, Dooku said, "It has come to my attention that Republic troops sighted a Mandalorian warrior on Vaced, despite the fact that I gave your sniper explicit instructions that secrecy was essential."

The Death Watch leader's helmet tilted forward as he said, "I am aware of the situation. It has been rectified."

"Rectified? How?"

"HoloNet News will report about a Corellian bounty hunter's body being discovered with the remains of a stolen ship that crashed on Vaced. The report will dismiss any question of Mandalorian involvement."

"And this 'Corellian bounty hunter' was really . . . ?"

"An available corpse."

"Very well," Dooku said. "But the next time I enlist your sniper, I insist he must exercise greater discretion."

The Death Watch leader nodded once. Dooku broke the connection, and the hologram flickered off. Dooku was already looking forward to his next conversation with the Mandalorian when he would inform him that the sniper had killed the wrong men and that Commissioner Sommilor and his pilots were still alive.

Remembering what Darth Sidious had said about Ring-Sol Ambase confronting Nuru Kungurama on Coruscant, Dooku smiled. He did not question Sidious's ability to foretell future events. He knew that the inevitable duel between Ambase and Kungurama would be glorious.

It never occurred to Dooku that Darth Sidious might have overlooked any loose ends.

CHAPTER 5

"This place stinks," Lalo Gunn said. "How much longer do we have to wait for the guy with the money to show up?"

The Duros bounty hunter Cad Bane took a slow sip from his glass, then replied, "Not long."

They were seated in the tavern at Vaced Spaceport. Night had fallen, and the tavern was crowded with locals. Most were talking about a swoop gang that had been blown to pieces by an explosion at the edge of the woods near the spaceport earlier that day. From the sporadic cheers and laughter, it sounded as if the swoop gang would not be missed.

Gunn raised her glass to her lips and emptied it. "Well, if you ask me, this transaction would have gone faster if *you'd* brought the credits."

"But I didn't ask you."

Gunn pushed her glass back and forth across the bar's crackled surface until the noise got the attention of the insectoid bartender, a male Vuvrian who had a broad head with twelve eyes and a pair of antennae that dangled down to his narrow shoulders. The bartender refilled Gunn's glass without comment. Gunn glanced at Bane and said, "As long as we're killing time, there's something I've been wondering about. Maybe you could clear it up for me."

Bane tilted his head forward, lowering his hat's wide brim over his red eyes. "What do you want to know?"

"On Kynachi, you hired me to make nice with the Jedi kid and his clone troopers and to stick close to them. They became Breakout Squad, I stuck with them, and then you sent a transmission, saying you'd pay me more to bring them to Vaced."

"Get to the point."

"After you contacted me, I got *another* transmission—you won't believe this—from

Chancellor Palpatine and some high-ranking Jedi named Yoda. Imagine my surprise when they said they wanted Breakout Squad to rendezvous with a Kynachi diplomat here on Vaced. At first, I thought, 'That's convenient,' because I didn't have to come up with an excuse to drop out of hyperspace to arrive in the Vaced system. But then I thought . . ."

"Yes?" Bane said, keeping his expression neutral.

"Well, you, Palpatine, and a senior Jedi, all wanting me to bring Breakout Squad to the same planet . . . seems like a mighty big coincidence."

Bane's expression did not change. "Are you implying that I'm working with the Chancellor and the Jedi Council?"

Gunn chuckled. "Don't get me wrong, friend, but I think they like to play with their own toy soldiers. However, you're a crafty one, you are. It wouldn't surprise me in the least if you were toying with *them*."

Gunn's compliment did not have any apparent effect on Bane. He took another sip of his drink.

"So what I was wondering," Gunn continued, "did you know the Kynachi diplomat was traveling to Coruscant? And did you pull strings to make the

Chancellor contact my ship so he would tell Breakout Squad to meet the diplomat on Vaced?"

"If I did pull any strings," Bane said, "that would be *my* business."

Gunn tilted her chair back but kept her hands on the bar, where Bane could see them. "Take it easy, friend. I was just asking." Looking away from Bane, she surveyed the other customers. "I'm sure glad I'm not stuck on Kynachi anymore, but I am going to miss my ship. It'll be tough to replace the *Hasty Harpy*."

Bane snickered. "Your ship was a rattletrap. With the money you've earned, you can buy a better rattletrap."

"My ship was running fine before the saboteur tampered with it."

"Saboteur? What saboteur?"

Gunn looked at Bane. During their conversation, she had picked up on a few subtle changes in his facial muscles and also slight vocal inflections that indicated he was keeping information to himself. Although she suspected Bane was a good liar, there was still a chance that he was unaware of any saboteurs on the *Hasty Harpy*. She replied, "All I know is someone planted a tracking device on the *Harpy*, rigged her navicomputer to send us to an uncharted black hole sector, and also activated her hypercomm after I'd switched it off. If I ever find out who was responsible, I'll blast him. Getting away from that black hole was no easy trick."

"Interesting." Bane lifted a gloved hand to stroke his chin. "Your only passengers were the Jedi, the clone troopers, and the droid. Did you suspect any of them?"

"One of the troopers seemed odd, and the droid was an odd one, but . . . oh, I don't know. No point in dwelling on it. The job is done, and the *Harpy*'s gone." She glanced at Bane and saw a small furrow form across his blue forehead. Perhaps he didn't know anything about a saboteur, she thought, but she wasn't about to take any chances.

Bane looked to the doorway and frowned. Gunn followed Bane's gaze and saw a short, amphibious alien, a Patrolian with mottled mauve scales, who carried a small satchel as he stepped through the tavern's entrance. Wide fins extended from either side of his head, and he wore a patch over his left eye. Gunn recognized him immediately.

The Patrolian saw Cad Bane and approached the bar. But when the Patrolian saw the woman seated beside Bane, his bulbous right eye widened and his mouth gaped open.

Gunn said, "So, you're the guy with the money, huh? I remember you, too." Turning to Bane, she continued, "Last time we met, he was with the crew of the Black Hole Pirates. Another big coincidence, huh?"

Bane shrugged.

Gunn returned her attention to the Patrolian and said, "I didn't know you two worked together, mister . . . wait, don't tell me." She reached out and patted the Patrolian's shoulder. "You're the one Captain McGrrrr called Robonino, right?"

Speaking in a wheezing croak, Robonino said, "McGrrrr is no longer my captain."

"You still traveling with Bossk?"

Robonino looked at Bane and said, "She asks a lot of questions."

Bane said, "I've noticed."

"Well, pardon me," Gunn said sourly. "I don't have anything against bounty hunters in general, but I'm making an exception for Bossk. If he's on Vaced,

I want to know about it because then I'll want to be leaving that much sooner."

Robonino laughed. "Stop worrying. Bossk is far from here." He handed the satchel to Bane.

Bane opened the satchel and removed a leather pouch that was filled with credit chips. He gave the pouch to Gunn and said, "Feel free to count it. It's all there."

"Why wouldn't it be?" Gunn said as she opened the bag to inspect the money.

"Stay put and have another drink," Bane said. "On me." He placed a small credit chip on the bar. "I'll be right back. I need a word with Robonino."

Bane and Robonino made their way through the crowded tavern and stepped outside into the moonlight. Looking around to make sure no one was listening, Bane said, "First of all, Doxun Feez was supposed to bring the money, not you. What happened to him?"

"Feez joined the McGrrrr Gang and asked me to bring the money to you."

Bane made a mental note to kill Doxun Feez if he ever saw him again, then said, "Second, when I gave you the coordinates to the Black Hole sector so you could infiltrate the McGrrrr Gang and make sure no harm came to anyone on the *Hasty Harpy*, I told you to bring backup. Why did you bring that fool Bossk?!"

"He was . . . available," Robonino said meekly. His eye twitched nervously as he recalled that he hadn't entirely protected the *Hasty Harpy*'s crew, especially after a droid named Cleaver had knocked him out cold. Robonino couldn't think of any good reason to mention this detail to Bane, so he didn't.

Bane scowled. "You're fortunate Bossk didn't bungle the job, bubble brain. Next time you subcontract, check with me before you—" Bane's words caught in his throat as he noticed a black metallic speck on Robonino's left shoulder. Bane leaned closer to see the speck was actually a small transmitter, and he remembered how Lalo Gunn had patted the Patrolian. He raised one finger in front of his mouth, signaling Robonino to stay silent as he used his other hand to pluck the transmitter free. He held the transmitter out for Robonino's inspection. Knowing that Gunn was probably still listening to them, Bane continued, "Did you hear a noise from behind that tree over there?"

Robonino looked at a dark, scraggy tree that grew nearby and said, "No, I didn't hear anything—"

Bane gave Robonino a quiet whack on the back of the head, then bent down and placed the transmitter on the ground. Robonino realized Bane was trying to create a diversion and said, "Yes! Yes, I did hear something."

"You wait here while I check it out," Bane said, but instead of walking toward the tree, he headed straight back to the tavern's entrance. He strode fast through the doorway, keeping both hands close to his holstered guns as he moved through the crowd and back to the bar.

Gunn was gone, her seat empty. The credit chip that Bane had left for her to buy another drink was right where he'd left it. He scanned the crowd and saw no one resembling Gunn. He looked back to the bar just in time to see the Vuvrian bartender reaching for the credit chip.

With remarkable speed, Bane's hand darted out, grabbed the bartender's thin wrist, and slammed it against the bar. The bartender yelped and was about to protest that he thought the credit chip was his tip when he lifted several of his eyes to meet the gaze of his attacker. Instead, he stared down the barrel of the large blaster that had appeared in the Duros's other hand.

"The woman who was sitting with me," Bane said. "Where'd she go?"

"I don't know!" the bartender cried. "I thought she left with you!"

Bane could tell the Vuvrian wasn't lying or pretending to be frightened out of his wits. The bounty hunter cursed under his breath as he released the bartender's hand. He snatched up the credit chip, pocketed it, and headed back for the door. Stepping outside, he found Robonino standing beside the transmitter. Bane crushed the transmitter under his boot, then said, "Did you see her come out?"

Robonino shook his head. "She must have left through the kitchen. She couldn't have gotten far."

Bane assumed Gunn had heard everything about him sending Robonino to the Black Hole sector to monitor Breakout Squad. At least she remained ignorant of the identity of his client, who'd supplied him with the Black Hole's coordinates and information about the McGrrrr Gang. Not even Robonino knew about Bane's client. Bane said, "She doesn't know anything damaging. But when people spy on me, I take it personally. We'll search the—"

Bane was interrupted by his chirping holocomm. He removed the holocomm from his belt, glanced at Robonino, and said, "I need to take this call. Stay put and watch for Gunn."

Bane walked away from the tavern and entered a dark alley, where he activated the holocomm. A hologram of a hooded man appeared in the air. The hooded man had previously hired Bane to capture Ring-Sol Ambase on Kynachi.

Darth Sidious rasped, "You are still on Vaced, bounty hunter?"

"I am."

"I have an assignment for you. It requires that you leave Vaced immediately."

Because Bane was more interested in a job that paid money than revenge against Lalo Gunn, he said, "I'm listening."

"The Jedi Ring-Sol Ambase and the clone trooper that you delivered to Bogg 5 . . . they have recovered, and they're on the loose. They are traveling in a Kuat *Corona*-class freighter, on their way to Coruscant as we speak. Ambase is under the impression that he cannot trust his fellow Jedi. I anticipate he will attempt to break into the Jedi Archives."

Bane was surprised to be offered another assignment that involved Ring-Sol Ambase, but he knew that his client's money was good. He said, "You want me to kill Ambase this time?"

"On the contrary," Sidious said. "I want you to help him."

Lalo Gunn knew it would have been a mistake to try running from the Duros bounty hunter, which was why she had taken the precaution of paying the tavern's assistant bartender a generous fee in exchange for concealing her in the tavern's storeroom. Hunkered down behind two large crates filled with nonperishable food, Gunn aimed her blaster at the room's only door.

Although the storeroom's lights were off, she could see a sliver of light along the door's left side. The assistant bartender, a Xexto, was supposed to rap four times on the door after the bounty hunter left, then he would enter the storeroom to show he was alone. If the Xexto thought Gunn was in danger, he would knock only three times as a warning.

If the Xexto tried to double-cross her and sent the bounty hunter into the storeroom, she would do her best to make them both regret it.

Almost thirty minutes passed before Gunn heard four raps against the other side of the door. Her finger tensed slightly against her blaster's trigger as the door slid open to reveal the Xexto's spindly silhouette, illuminated by the light from the hallway behind him. A four-armed alien with a small head that bobbed at the top of a long, thin neck, the Xexto cautiously stepped into the room and was reaching for a switch on the wall when Gunn said, "Don't touch the lights—and hands where I can see them."

The Xexto lifted all four hands. "The Duros is gone," he said, "along with his fishy friend."

Gunn didn't budge from her position as she said, "How long?"

"About ten minutes. They both left in a freighter. I watched them board. Saw the freighter lift off."

"Turn on the lights and step back through the door."

The Xexto chuckled as he lowered his hands and tapped the light switch, then walked back through the doorway to stand in the outer hallway. Gunn lowered her blaster but kept it in her grip as she eased herself out from behind the crates. With her free hand, she tossed a credit chip through the doorway to the Xexto. The Xexto caught the chip with his upper left hand and said, "You keep throwing money at me, and I'll keep helping you. Something else you need?"

"An introduction," Gunn said. "I want to meet your local starship dealer. I'm in a buying mood for a rattletrap."

CHAPTER 6

Nuru Kungurama stepped through a narrow doorway and entered a wide, dark room. Although Nuru couldn't see a light source and the undecorated walls and high ceiling were without windows, long shadows slithered like serpents across the bare floor. At first, Nuru thought he was the only person in the room, but then he saw a lone robed figure standing against the far wall. The figure was a tall man with silver hair.

A chill traveled up Nuru's spine as he recognized Ring-Sol Ambase.

"You never should have left the Jedi Temple, young one," Ambase said. "You never should have followed me." Ambase appeared to glide slowly away from the wall, moving toward Nuru as if his feet were not in direct contact with the floor.

Nuru took a cautious step backward as he moved his hand toward his belt. His hand stopped short as he felt the intensity of Ambase's gaze locking onto the second lightsaber that dangled from his belt.

Ambase said, "I see you have something that doesn't belong to you."

A loud rush of wind blasted across the room, and the walls and ceiling vanished, revealing an expansive view of towering buildings and spires that surrounded Nuru's position. Nuru suddenly realized he was not in a room at all, but that he was standing on a skyscraper's roof in an unfamiliar area on the planet Coruscant.

He became aware of other figures on the roof. Two clone troopers and a skeletal droid were fighting. He thought the clones were attacking the droid, but then one clone hit the other while the droid just watched.

While the clones continued their fight, the distant clouds behind Ambase began to churn, generating low rumbles of thunder. Lightning flashed, igniting the mirrored windows of a nearby skyscraper that resembled a raised sword. Ambase moved closer to Nuru, extended one hand forward, and said, "The lightsabers. Give them to me."

Nuru shook his head. "No, M—" He choked back on the word *Master*. The man who stood before him was no longer his Master, no longer a Jedi. To Nuru, he was the man who'd blasted Veeren's ship to pieces. A killer.

"I'm no killer," Ambase said. "And I *am* your Master."

Nuru didn't know how Ambase was reading his thoughts. He tried to calm his mind, to remember his Jedi training, but he was distracted by the fighting clones and his own simmering emotions.

"I can feel your anger," Ambase said. He held out both hands, exposing his palms. "I am defenseless. It's your move."

Nuru thought again of Veeren, how he had watched helplessly as her ship exploded. He felt a violent surge of power course through his veins. Baring his teeth, he grabbed for his lightsaber.

But his lightsaber was gone, along with his Master's weapon. And as his hand clutched the empty air beside his belt, he saw both lightsabers materialize instantly in Ambase's hands.

Ambase ignited the lightsabers. He crossed the humming blades of energy in front of him, swept them across each other, and the blades made a crackling noise as they scissored toward Nuru's head.

"NO!" Nuru shouted as he opened his eyes.

"Are you all right, Commander?" Breaker said.

Nuru was seated beside Breaker, behind the two KynachTech pilots, Pikkson and Sunmantle, in the cockpit of the Suwantek freighter. Through the cockpit's windows, he saw the cascade of luminous streaks that indicated the ship was still traveling through hyperspace. The pilots had swiveled their seats to glance back at Nuru, who had one hand placed firmly across the two lightsabers at his belt. Nuru blinked his red eyes as he removed his hand from the weapons. "Sorry," he said. "I had a bad dream."

"Oh," Breaker said. "I didn't know you ever had bad dreams."

"I didn't, either." Squirming in his seat, Nuru said, "Is everything all right with the ship and passengers?"

"The ship is operating fine, sir," Sunmantle said.

Breaker said, "Do you want a status report, sir?"

"Yes, please."

"Commissioner Sommilor is resting in the crew quarters. Chatterbox is still unconscious but stable. Umbrag remains locked up. Cleaver's guarding him."

"Good," Nuru said. "I guess I'm just . . . anxious."

The pilots returned their attention to the ship's controls. Breaker leaned closer to Nuru and whispered, "Commander, you really do look rattled. If you don't mind my asking . . . about your dream?"

"I saw Ring-Sol Ambase. He was on Coruscant. He tried to kill me."

Breaker's brow furrowed. "When we were on Kynachi, you said the reason you left the Jedi Temple and followed Ambase was because you had a feeling that something might go wrong with his mission. And you were right. Everything went very wrong. Could your dream be like that feeling you had? A prediction of what will happen?"

"I don't know." Nuru shook his head. "I'm not certain of very much anymore. Nothing has gone as expected since I left the temple."

Breaker sighed. "I began my life in a vat in Kamino ten years ago, which makes me younger than you, sir. And I'm just a soldier without special powers, and I'll never be as wise as a Jedi. But if there's one thing I can tell you, it's that everything doesn't always go according to plan. You have to be ready to improvise. And while you may feel uncertain about many things, Commander, you can trust that the boys and I would gladly follow you anywhere."

Nuru smiled and said, "Thank you, Breaker." He still felt uneasy about his dream of Ambase. He leaned forward in his seat, tapped Pikkson's shoulder, and said, "When do we exit hyperspace?"

"Twenty minutes, sir."

Breaker said, "I'm sure you'll feel better when you return to the temple."

"You're probably right," Nuru said as he rose from his seat. "Let's check on Chatterbox and the others."

Leaving his helmet on a hook at the back of his seat, Breaker followed Nuru out of the cockpit. Nuru tried to calm his thoughts, but he could not shake the feeling that something bad was about to happen.

Knuckles and Gizz were sitting with the trooper they called Sharp in the main hold of the Suwantek freighter, a short distance from where Cleaver stood outside the hatch of the chamber that held Umbrag. Because Gizz was in desperate need of a shower but refused to take one, Knuckles had suggested that he and Sharp wear their helmets, which had built-in air purifiers. This was a relief to the impersonator because it was physically tiring for the Clawdite to maintain his appearance for prolonged periods.

But even after the Clawdite had relaxed his facial muscles, he was not breathing easily. He was worried about Asajj Ventress and what she might want him to do next.

He had already sabotaged the life pods on the starship that carried Ring-Sol Ambase to Kynachi. On Kynachi, Ventress had ambushed Sharp to allow the Clawdite to impersonate Sharp and infiltrate Breakout Squad. The Clawdite then rigged Lalo Gunn's ship to go to the Black Hole sector and activated the ship's hypercomm to enable interstellar communication while traveling through hyperspace. He had done all these things because if he hadn't, Ventress would kill him.

When he had last spoken with Ventress, she had told him to contact her in one hour, but that hour had long passed. Traveling through hyperspace without any access to a hypercomm transmitter, he wouldn't be able to talk with her again on his own holocomm until he reached Coruscant. He knew she would be furious. As for what the clones would do to him if they discovered he were a Clawdite, he could only imagine.

"Something wrong, Sharp?" Knuckles said. "You've been awfully quiet."

"I'm worried about Chatterbox," the Clawdite said.

Nuru and Breaker walked into the hold. Breaker said, "We just checked in on Chatterbox and Quills. Chatterbox's condition remains stable." Looking from Knuckles to Sharp, Breaker said, "Why are you wearing your helmets?" But then his nostrils flared and he looked at Gizz, and Breaker added, "Never mind."

Nuru said, "We'll be exiting hyperspace in about ten minutes." He looked at the droid standing on the other side of the hold. "Cleaver, make sure Umbrag hasn't tried to remove his restraints."

Cleaver opened the hatch for the chamber that held Umbrag. The droid stepped into the chamber and said, "Commander! Something's wrong."

Nuru ran into the chamber and found Cleaver kneeling beside Umbrag, who was lying on his side on the deck. From what Nuru could see, the binder cuffs were still firmly in place around Umbrag's wrists and ankles. Umbrag wasn't moving.

Nuru dropped down beside Cleaver and looked at the green flesh at the top and back of Umbrag's head. When he couldn't detect any sign of a pulse, he examined the pressure controls on Umbrag's metal chest plate. Breaker, Knuckles, and Sharp moved to the chamber's hatch in time to hear Nuru ask, "Is his breathing apparatus working?"

"I'm not certain," Cleaver said. "Perhaps he switched it off?"

Gizz moved up behind the troopers outside the chamber and said, "What's going on in there?"

Ignoring Gizz, Nuru glanced back at the hatch so he could face the troopers and said, "Get a med kit and a tool kit, and also get Quills!" The three troopers shoved past Gizz, who stumbled backward. As the troopers ran off in different directions,

Nuru was returning his attention to Umbrag when something hard smashed against the side of his head.

Umbrag had been faking unconsciousness and had waited for exactly the right moment to swing both arms at Nuru. As Nuru fell sideways to the deck, Umbrag lifted his own upper body fast, clamped his manacled gauntlets around the young Jedi's head, and rolled away from Cleaver.

Cleaver prepared to launch himself at Umbrag, but when Umbrag's back hit the opposite bulkhead, the Skakoan was holding Nuru like a small shield against his chest, his forearms braced across Nuru's throat. Through his armored suit's vocalizer, Umbrag wheezed mechanically, "One wrong move and I'll break the Jedi's neck!"

Cleaver froze. Nuru's eyes were closed, and his body was limp. From the open hatch, Gizz bellowed, "Let go of the kid, you ugly—!"

Overseer Umbrag twisted his wrists slightly, simultaneously applying pressure to Nuru's neck while firing a bolt of energy from a concealed blaster in his left gauntlet. The bolt smashed into Gizz's upper chest, knocking the giant backward into the main hold.

Cleaver was still poised to attack when he realized Umbrag had twisted his concealed weapon so its barrel was braced against the bottom of Nuru's jaw. Cleaver heard one of the troopers yell outside the chamber. Umbrag kept his own eyes fixed on the droid as he said, "I'll kill the boy unless you do as I say!"

Cleaver said, "Nuru Kungurama isn't the only Jedi on board."

"What?!"

Cleaver had been hoping to distract Umbrag, and when he heard the surprise in Umbrag's voice, he knew his bluff had worked.

The droid automatically calculated the movements of the troopers outside the hatch and simultaneously calculated how he would leap across the chamber, grab Umbrag's gauntlets, and rescue Nuru. But just as Cleaver sprang toward Umbrag, he heard a second round of blaster fire tear into the chamber.

The shot came from the hatch. Cleaver was still traveling through the air when he saw the fired energy bolt race toward Umbrag and hit the only unprotected area of the Skakoan's armored body.

A millisecond after the impact, Cleaver grabbed Umbrag's gauntlets and pulled them toward his own metal body to prevent the gauntlet blaster from harming anyone else. The droid twisted in midair so his feet landed on the deck as he yanked the gauntlets free.

Umbrag had been killed instantly. Cleaver checked to make sure Nuru was still breathing, then turned his metal head to gaze at the open hatch. He saw Sharp standing above Gizz's fallen body in the doorway. Sharp's feet were braced between Gizz's sprawled legs, and he held his blaster rifle so it was still aimed at Umbrag's head. Behind Sharp, Knuckles and Breaker held their own rifles.

Still facing Sharp, Cleaver said, "You moved faster than I calculated."

The Clawdite stammered, "Is the commander all right?"

Gizz groaned loudly from the deck. As Knuckles knelt beside Gizz, Breaker leaped past Sharp and into the chamber. Dropping beside Nuru and pulling him away from Umbrag, Breaker cupped the back of Nuru's head and said, "Can you hear me, sir?" He lowered his ear over the boy's mouth, then said, "He's out cold, but breathing fine." As he scooped up Nuru and carried him out through the hatch, he said, "No one touches Umbrag. Seal the chamber."

Cleaver followed Breaker out of the chamber and sealed the hatch. Knuckles said, "Gizz! You still with us?"

"Yeah," Gizz muttered as he shifted his bulk against the deck. "Takes more than one blaster bolt to kill me dead. But I think I could use a med kit. How's Umbrag?"

"He won't be needing a med kit."

Gizz grinned. "This day just keeps getting better."

While Knuckles opened a med kit and began cleaning Gizz's wound, Cleaver stared hard at Sharp and said, "I calculated I could rescue the commander without any loss of life. How did you move so fast?"

The Clawdite said, "I don't know. I just . . . moved."

Knuckles said, "Let's just be glad Nuru is all right, that Umbrag didn't hurt him. I can't believe how Umbrag took us all by surprise."

Cleaver said, "Perhaps if I'd moved faster . . ."

"Maybe you should have Breaker check your circuits," Knuckles said.

Cleaver shook his head sadly. "Maybe I'm just not cut out to be a Jedi."

Nuru was dimly aware of the sound of the Suwantek freighter's sublight engines kicking in when he opened his eyes to see Breaker and Quills standing above him.

From the way they were looming over him, he could tell he was lying on an elevated bunk in the crew's quarters. Quills was studying a small medical scanner that he held a few centimeters away from Nuru's head.

Nuru said, "What . . . where are we?"

"Easy, Commander," Quills said. "You were unconscious for several minutes."

"We've left hyperspace?"

"Yes, sir," Breaker said.

Nuru took a deep breath. "How close are we to Coruscant?"

"We just reached orbit."

Nuru squeezed his eyes closed. He opened them again. "Did Umbrag hit me?"

"He did, sir. Just before he locked you in a stranglehold."

"Oh," Nuru said, rubbing his neck. "I guess I didn't stop him."

Breaker scowled. "The boys and I did a lousy job of watching your back, sir. It's my fault. I should have inspected Umbrag's armor more carefully when we put the binders on him. He had a blaster built into one of his gauntlets. After he knocked you out, he shot Gizz, and—"

"Gizz?!"

"He's all right, sir."

Quills nodded in agreement. "I slapped a bacta patch on the big fellow. He'll be fine, but I should go check on him and Chatterbox."

Thinking fast, Nuru said, "Tell the pilots to take us directly to the Galactic Senate building. We need to deliver the commissioner there before we bring Chatterbox for treatment at the Jedi Temple."

"Aye, sir," Quills said. He exited the crew's quarters.

Nuru looked at Breaker and said, "Why did Umbrag wait until we'd almost reached Coruscant before he attacked?"

"I wondered the same thing. Maybe he just panicked. If he had a reason, he took it with him."

"What do you mean?"

"Umbrag had his gauntlet blaster up against your neck, sir. Sharp shot him. He's dead."

"Oh." Nuru felt slightly ill as he pushed himself up so he rested on his elbows. "That's unfortunate."

"He could have killed you. Sharp saved your life."

"I'm grateful for that, but I'm also sure the Jedi Council and Galactic Senate would have preferred Umbrag still alive so he could have been interrogated." Nuru checked his belt to make sure Ring-Sol Ambase's lightsaber was still secured beside his own. "Where's Umbrag's body?"

"Sealed in the chamber where he attacked you."

Nuru grimaced. "I need to see it. After we deliver Commissioner Sommilor to the Senate, I expect I'll have to make a full report to the Jedi Council."

Breaker followed Nuru out of the crew's quarters, and they headed for the main hold. "Commander, if what Aristocra said about spies and assassins being everywhere is true, how can we be sure you'll be safe anywhere on Coruscant?"

Nuru sighed. "We'll just have to stay alert and take our chances."

"That's not exactly what I'd call a plan."

"No, it's not. But as you said, everything doesn't always go according to plan."

Breaker shook his head. "I wish you hadn't reminded me."

The Suwantek freighter was still descending through Coruscant's atmosphere, heading for the Galactic Senate building, when a Kuat *Corona*-class transport dropped out of hyperspace in the Coruscant system.

Because thousands of other ships were always arriving at or departing from the heavily populated planet at any given time, no one took any special notice of the *Corona*.

Inside the *Corona*, the clone trooper named Sharp turned to Ring-Sol Ambase and said, "Do you want to go straight to the Dacho District, General?"

Ambase nodded.

Sharp reached for the flight controls but hesitated. "If I may ask, sir . . . how do you know Dooku isn't leading us into a trap?"

"I *don't* know," Ambase said. "But he could have killed us easily before we left his palace, and he didn't. So take us down, Sharp, and use stealth. We must not alert other Jedi to our presence."

Sharp punched the *Corona*'s thrusters and moved into the shadow of a passenger carrier that was heading in the general direction of the Dacho District.

While the *Corona* approached a sprawl of industrial skyscrapers that made up the Coruscant's Dacho District, a battered-looking Telgorn dropship exited hyperspace and angled toward the night side of Coruscant.

The dropship's name was the *Sleight of Hand*, and despite her appearance, she carried heavily modified weapons and defensive systems. Her owner was Cad Bane.

Bane sat in the cockpit alongside Robonino. Robonino said, "You're certain your client hired you to *help* a Jedi?"

"If I weren't certain," Bane drawled, "we wouldn't have left Vaced in such a hurry." He tapped at a keypad, entering data that had been transmitted by his client. A scope displayed a graphic readout of an industrial sector on Coruscant, then a green blip appeared, along with a string of numbers. The blip represented a starship, and the numbers were the ship's identification code. Bane said, "Got him."

Robonino's fins bent back against the side of his head. "Got who?"

"The Jedi, Ring-Sol Ambase. He's traveling in a Kuat transport over the Dacho District. Looks like he's going to land at Moxonnic Manufacturing, or rather what's left of the place." Bane steered the dropship down through Coruscant's night sky as he plotted a course for the abandoned facility. "It will be interesting to see him again."

Robonino's eyeball rolled with surprise. "You've met this Jedi before?"

"He wasn't conscious at the time," Bane said. "That's why seeing him again will be interesting."

CHAPTER 7

The Galactic Senate building was an immense, elevated, dome-shaped structure, which rested on a cylindrical foundation in the heart of Coruscant's densely populated government district. After Nuru Kungurama directed the Kynachi pilots to land the Suwantek freighter inside one of the building's many hangars, he went to the main hold where Commissioner Sommilor stood waiting with Breaker, Knuckles, Gizz, and Cleaver. Nuru said, "Gizz and Cleaver, you'll remain on board while we bring the commissioner to the Senate rotunda."

"Yes, Commander," Cleaver said.

Gizz said, "How come I gotta stay on board?"

Nuru was afraid Gizz might deliberately or accidentally cause trouble in the Senate building, but he didn't want Gizz to know that. Thinking fast, he said, "Because I need you to make sure that the Kynachi pilots don't leave without us."

"Okay," Gizz said as he cracked his knuckles. "But don't take too long. I'm getting hungry again."

Nuru faced Breaker and Knuckles and said, "Where's Sharp?"

"In the 'fresher," Knuckles said. "He said he began feeling sick again during our descent."

Breaker said, "I'll make sure Sharp gets a thorough examination when we return to the Jedi Temple."

"Fine," Nuru said. "Sharp can remain on board. Now then, Commissioner, are you ready?"

Sommilor beamed proudly. "Indeed I am."

Disguised as Sharp, the Clawdite shape-shifter peeked outside the hatch of the refresher station inside the Suwantek freighter. After confirming that no one was standing outside the 'fresher, the Clawdite shut the hatch and relaxed his facial muscles to revert to his natural state, then activated his holocomm unit to contact Asajj Ventress.

Several seconds passed before Ventress's angry face materialized as a hologram in front of the Clawdite. Ventress said, "You're late."

"I couldn't help it! We left Bilbringi and jumped to hyperspace and—"

"Where are you?"

"Coruscant."

"Listen carefully," Ventress said. "Umbrag is important to the Separatists. You will help him escape and bring him to me."

The Clawdite gasped. "Help him?! But he's—"

"Do it!" Ventress broke the connection, and her hologram vanished.

The Clawdite stared at his holocomm unit. His lower lip trembled as he muttered, "I'm dead."

Nuru led Sommilor, Breaker, and Knuckles out of the freighter and down the landing ramp. As they walked toward a lift tube that would take them to the rotunda where the Senate meetings were held, Nuru was surprised to see Supreme Chancellor Palpatine, his guards, and a tall alien Jedi stepping away from a sleek shuttle. The Jedi was a male Anx, a large reptilian alien with a high, tapered head and long, pointed chin.

Palpatine saw Nuru, too. "Nuru Kungurama? At last, we meet in person." Then Palpatine looked to Sommilor and smiled as he said, "Ah, Commissioner Sommilor. Welcome to Coruscant."

Sommilor bowed. "Thank you, Chancellor."

"This is an amazing coincidence," Palpatine said. He gestured to the Anx Jedi and said, "Nuru Kungurama, I assume you're acquainted with the Jedi scholar Harro Kelpura? Master Kelpura was just telling me about his research."

"We've never met," Kelpura said in a low, rumbling voice as he bowed to Nuru. "I was distressed when I learned you left Coruscant, young one. I am glad you returned safely."

Nuru bowed in return. He had forgotten that Kit Fisto mentioned Kelpura to him on Bilbringi. "Master Fisto told me you've been studying the escape pod that—"

"Oh, but you must *see* it to appreciate what I've learned," Kelpura said. "I had to move the pod to my new research laboratory away from the Temple as a safety precaution, but there's really nothing to worry about. Except perhaps the discovery of a lifetime!"

Palpatine looked at Nuru and said, "I urge you to go with Master Kelpura. My guards and I will personally escort Commissioner Sommilor to the Senate meeting."

Sommilor thanked Nuru again before he walked off with Palpatine and the guards. Nuru turned to Kelpura and said, "I do want to see the escape pod, but we must return to the Jedi Temple first." He pointed to the Suwantek freighter. "I have an injured trooper who needs medical treatment."

"Then let's be on our way!" Kelpura said as he trotted toward the freighter.

Ring-Sol Ambase and the clone named Sharp sat inside the *Corona* transport, which they'd landed on a rooftop platform on a skyscraper in the Dacho District. Except for several airspeeders that moved across the sky in the distance, there were few signs of life in any direction, but this was not unusual. Several hundred years earlier, an immense industrial chemical accident had killed more than three hundred thousand beings in the area, and most of the buildings, factories, and warehouses in the Dacho District had been deserted ever since. The district was commonly referred to as the Dead Sector.

Sharp looked around at the surrounding rooftops. One nearby skyscraper had a sharply angled top that made the entire building resemble a raised sword and loomed over an old air-taxi hub. Sharp said, "Where's Dooku?"

The *Corona*'s holocomm chirped. Ambase pressed a button and a hologram of Count Dooku appeared. Ambase looked at the hologram and said, "Decided not to join us?"

"Traveling to Coruscant has proved more difficult for me than I anticipated," Dooku said. "I ran into some Weequay pirates. But I have not abandoned you, old friend. Stay where you are. Help is on the way, and I'll be there, too, as soon as I can."

"Help?" Ambase said. "What do you mean?"

Dooku's hologram began rapidly flickering.

"Something's jamming . . . signal and my . . . can't hear—" The hologram vanished.

Ambase and Sharp climbed out of the *Corona* and onto the rooftop platform. Ambase looked up and saw a small, battered ship descending toward them. Sharp saw the ship, too, and said, "Recognize it?"

"A Telgorn dropship."

The dropship landed on the roof about twenty meters from the *Corona*. Ambase and Sharp watched as a Duros and a Patrolian climbed out of the dropship. The Duros wore a broad-brimmed hat and a long coat, and his belt held a pair of blasters. He carried a satchel in one hand and had what appeared to be weapon-laden gauntlets wrapped around both forearms. The Patrolian's left eye was covered by a patch, and a padded backpack was slung across his small back.

Sharp whispered, "Bounty hunters?"

"Looks like it," Ambase said.

Walking slowly across the roof, Cad Bane and Robonino approached the Jedi and the clone trooper. Bane said, "Ring-Sol Ambase."

Surprised, Ambase said, "I don't believe we've met."

Bane grinned. "I'm working for a client who prefers to remain anonymous. He told me to meet you here." Bane aimed a thumb at Robonino and added, "My associate and I are to assist you."

Ambase said, "Did your client tell you *how* you might assist me?"

"You're looking to obtain an exotic escape pod that's in this building. My associate and I have access codes and equipment to get you past the building's security systems. You'll need us to help you get the pod out of the building and onto your ship." Bane put down the satchel he'd been carrying, then kicked it so it skidded a short distance across the rooftop before it came to a stop in front of Ambase. Bane said, "Inside the bag, you'll find a pair of Republic Navy officers' uniforms. Put them on. The uniforms will allow you and the clone to get past the guards who are stationed inside."

Ambase said, "I have some experience with infiltrating buildings. In case your client didn't tell you, I'm a Jedi."

Bane smiled. "I don't hold that against you.

But from what I've heard, even a Jedi can use help, especially if he's lost his lightsaber."

Sharp glared at the Duros as he moved in front of Ambase and said, "How do *you* know General Ambase isn't carrying a lightsaber?"

Keeping his eyes on Ambase, Bane said, "Because I happened to be on Kynachi during the liberation, and it's my understanding that another Jedi took your weapon. I heard the Jedi was a blue-skinned boy. Know him?"

Ambase sensed the Duros was dangerous but did not sense he was lying. He looked at Sharp, then looked back at the Duros. "We're wasting time," he said as he picked up the satchel. "We'll change clothes inside, and then you'll take us to the escape pod."

Bane grinned. He knew from experience that it was usually best not to tell an outright lie to a Jedi. The reason he was certain that Nuru Kungurama left Kynachi with Ambase's weapon was because Bane had been the one who'd handed it to him.

The Suwantek freighter climbed away from the Galactic Senate building. Inside the freighter's main hold, Nuru Kungurama was introducing Harro Kelpura to Gizz and Cleaver when an alarm chirped from a small box-shaped datapad on Kelpura's belt.

"What's this?" Kelpura plucked the device from his belt and flipped it open to display a datascreen. "Must be some kind of technical error." He adjusted the image on the screen, and his large eyes went wide with surprise. Turning his tapered head to face Nuru, he said, "We must change course for the Dacho District this instant."

Nuru said, "Master Kelpura, I know you're eager to show me the escape pod, but—"

"Change course *now*," Kelpura said. He held out the datapad so Nuru could look at its screen. "Two ships have landed without authorization on my lab building's roof, and the alarm system has been disabled. Someone must be trying to steal the pod!"

Examining the datascreen, Nuru saw that one of the ships was a *Corona*-class transport.

Ambase.

Nuru grabbed the datapad and shoved it into a

socket. He pressed a button and said, "Kungurama to the bridge. Get a lock on the location of this building in the Dacho District and take us there now."

The pilots obeyed. As the freighter dropped out of its flight path to the temple and angled off toward the Dacho District, Cleaver said, "But, Commander Kungurama . . . shouldn't we take Chatterbox to a medical—?"

"We'll get him to the temple as soon as we can," Nuru interrupted. "Master Kelpura, I have reason to believe my Master, Ring-Sol Ambase, is already at your laboratory."

"Really?" Kelpura said. "That's good news!"

"No, it isn't," Nuru said, "because I don't think Ambase is on our side anymore."

No alarms sounded within the building that had been converted to Kelpura's research laboratory. Walking ahead of Bane, Ambase, and Sharp, Robonino made quick work of unlocking doors and deactivating sensors as they moved deeper into the building.

Both Ambase and Sharp were wearing the dark gray uniforms and black leather boots of Republic Navy officers. Ambase's uniform had a rank badge that identified him as an admiral. Sharp's badge identified him as a commander.

They soon arrived at a makeshift checkpoint where four human guards were stationed outside a large, locked door. Seeing a Republic admiral approach, the guards snapped to attention, opened the door, and allowed the group to pass. If the guards thought it odd that a Republic officer and clone trooper were accompanied by a menacing-looking Duros and Patrolian, they didn't see fit to mention it.

The door closed behind Ambase's group. Robonino immediately reached into his backpack, pulled out a magna lock, and slapped it across the door so it would be impossible to open from the other side. Bane said, "No way for the guards to follow us now."

Sharp said, "I'm guessing we won't be leaving the way we came."

"You guess right," Bane said. They proceeded through another corridor. Bane pointed to a connecting corridor and said, "We turn left here, and we should arrive at the entrance of the room where the pod's kept." But when they turned left, they arrived upon the unexpected.

"Sentry droids?" Robonino muttered as he observed the three weapon-laden automatons that stood before a large, metal door. He glanced at Bane with his one good eye. "Your client say anything about them?"

"No," Bane said. "They must be new. Just keep walking toward them so they don't suspect anything."

Seeing the four figures approach, one droid stepped away from the others and said, "Halt."

Bane's right hand made a casual dip to his holster. He brought the blaster pistol up fast and shot the droid twice through the head. The two remaining droids made rapid clicking sounds as they lurched forward and trained their own weapons at Bane, but Bane's left hand had already yanked his other blaster out. He squeezed the triggers of both blasters at the same time, and he fired again. The droids' heads exploded simultaneously, and all three droids collapsed to the floor like broken puppets.

"So much for doing things quietly," Bane said. He looked at Robonino, tilted his head toward the metal door, and said, "Open it."

Robonino reached into his backpack again and pulled out two small thermal detonators with magnetic edges. While Bane motioned Ambase and Sharp to follow him back into the adjoining corridor, Robonino planted the two detonators on the metal door, then walked quickly to catch up with the others.

The explosion was very loud.

The dust was still settling as Bane and Robonino returned to the door, or rather what was left of it. Ambase and Sharp followed the bounty hunters and saw a gaping, shredded rupture in the middle of the door. Bane led the way through the rupture.

The laboratory had a high ceiling that was laced with metal pipes and exhaust fans. Narrow windows lined the upper walls. At the center of the lab, a cluster of computers and sensor-laden equipment surrounded a wide platform. On the platform rested a small teardrop-shaped spacecraft.

Ambase felt his throat go dry at the sight of the Chiss escape pod. He hadn't seen it in over a decade, but it looked exactly as he'd remembered. He spotted its most distinguishing feature, the triangular egress hatch that lacked grips or latches, and he remembered how he and Dooku had squeezed into the pod to remove the infant Nuru Kungurama.

Bane looked at Ambase and said, "Something wrong?"

Ambase shook his head. "No."

"Then let's get this done," Bane said. He began tapping at the keypad on the back of one of his gauntlets while Robonino went to the far wall and began planting more explosives.

Ambase looked at Bane and said, "What are you doing?"

"Powering up my ship," Bane said as he stopped tapping his gauntlet. "After my associate blows the wall, the autopilot will bring my ship to us."

Sharp said, "You're going to use a tractor beam to yank the pod out of here?"

"Right again," Bane said. "And then we'll transfer the pod to your transport, and you can take it away."

Ambase said, "Take it away *where*?"

Bane shrugged. "I was only paid to make sure you got the pod. After that, you can take it wherever you want."

By the time the Suwantek freighter had left Coruscant's Senate District and entered the Dacho District, Nuru and Breaker had moved to the seats behind the pilots in the bridge. They had a clear view of the abandoned factories and skyscrapers, and when Nuru saw the gleaming building that resembled a raised sword, he felt his stomach clench. "Breaker, that building . . . I saw it in my dream."

"The dream you had of Ambase?"

Nuru nodded. The pilots guided the Suwantek toward the laboratory building on which they saw a *Corona*-class transport and a Telgorn dropship resting on the roof.

Breaker said, "How did the dream end?"

"Ambase killed me."

The Suwantek was still descending toward the laboratory building when a large section of the building's west wall exploded.

CHAPTER 8

The Kynachi pilots, Pikkson and Sunmantle, swung the Suwantek freighter away from the laboratory building to avoid the explosion's spray of fire and smoke. Sunmantle swatted the ship's intercom button and said, "Everyone buckle up and hold tight!"

Nuru leaned forward so his head was beside Pikkson's and said, "Are any life-forms in the ships on the roof?"

Pikkson consulted a sensor and said, "No, sir."

"Then circle back and put us down."

The pilots obeyed, steering the Suwantek through a wide curve around the eastern side of the building. Behind Nuru, Harro Kelpura poked his large head through the bridge's hatch and said, "What happened?"

"Big explosion," Nuru said. "Please return to your seat, Master Kelpura."

Kelpura stumbled away from the hatch. The Suwantek angled up for the rooftop, leveled off, and was about to land when the Telgorn dropship leaped unexpectedly from the roof and smashed into the Suwantek's aft thrusters, knocking the freighter sideways.

The Suwantek's engines whined as the pilots struggled with controls, trying to right the vessel. Breaker threw one arm protectively in front of Nuru as the freighter lost altitude and traveled over a chasm between skyscrapers. Sunmantle said, "We're going down!"

As Nuru sensed the approaching impact, he suddenly thought of Chatterbox, lying unconscious and defenseless in the Suwantek. He regretted that he hadn't delivered the wounded trooper to the Jedi Temple as soon as they'd arrived on Coruscant, and he felt a sense of failure. All he could do was hope that his allies would survive.

And then the Suwantek freighter crashed.

A cold wind rushed in through the large hole that exploded out from the west side of the laboratory building. Inside the remains of the laboratory, Ring-Sol Ambase, Sharp, and Robonino stood near the undamaged Chiss escape pod, while Cad Bane guided his dropship in through the blasted hole. Because of the dropship's powerful deflector shields, the ship was not only undamaged by the collision with the Suwantek freighter, but Bane didn't even realize there'd been a collision.

As the ship touched down on the lab's floor, Bane glanced at Sharp and Robonino and said, "You two, clear a path for the tractor beam."

Sharp and Robonino went to the computers and other equipment that had been set up around the escape pod, and they began shoving aside all the apparatuses that lay between the pod and the dropship.

Ambase stepped closer to the pod, examined the base that it rested on, and then turned to Bane and said, "There's a Jedi energy lock securing the pod to the floor. Only a Force user can unlock it."

"Then do your stuff, Jedi," Bane said before he climbed into the dropship.

Ambase found the energy lock's control panel and placed his right palm against it. A humming sound emanated from the base, followed by a muffled pop. Satisfied that the pod had been freed from its energized mooring, Ambase stepped away from the pod.

Bane activated the dropship's tractor beam and aimed it at the pod. As the beam lifted the pod and drew it closer to the dropship, Robonino gestured to Ambase and Sharp to follow him into the dropship. After they boarded, Bane backed the dropship out through the hole in the lab's wall, taking the pod with it, and ascended to the building's roof.

"Breaker. Breaker! Are you all right?"

Breaker groaned. He and Nuru were still belted into their seats in the Suwantek's bridge. The Suwantek had plowed sideways into a tangle of ventilation pipes that covered the roof of an abandoned building and had come to a stop near the edge of the roof. The bridge's lights were still on, but the ship's engine had died. Breaker had a bloody gash on the side of his jaw.

"Breaker?!"

Breaker opened his eyes. "I hear you, Commander. I'm with you."

"Go check on the others."

While Breaker scrambled out of his seat, Nuru unbuckled his safety belt and peered past Pikkson and Sunmantle so he could see the laboratory building in the distance. He looked just in time to see the Telgorn dropship rising up to the roof along with a small, teardrop-shaped escape pod.

Nuru shouted, "Sunmantle! Pikkson!"

"Yes, sir?" Pikkson said.

"Can you get this ship airborne?"

Pikkson consulted a status readout and said, "We lost one thruster, but I think we can—"

"Do it! Now!"

Pikkson punched the ignition for the repulsorlift engines, and the freighter began to rise from the roof's crushed ventilation pipes. But then the freighter shuddered and Sunmantle said, "Something's snagged our landing gear."

"I'll take care of it," Nuru said. He pointed to the lab building. "The moment we're free, make a close pass over that roof so I can jump to it." He turned and bolted out of the bridge and almost ran straight into Breaker.

"Quills and Chatterbox are okay," Breaker said as he followed Nuru to the main hold. "I think Sharp's trapped in the 'fresher."

Entering the main hold, Nuru saw the passengers had taken a pounding. The visor on Knuckles's helmet was cracked. Harro Kelpura was sprawled across the deck. Cleaver's left arm was bent at an odd angle. Gizz had accidentally slammed into a bulkhead and left a large dent.

Knuckles moved beside Harro Kelpura, touched the Anx's neck, and said, "Master Kelpura was knocked out."

Gizz rubbed the back of his head, looked at Nuru, and said, "What in blazes happened, kid?"

"We crashed, and our landing gear is snagged." He popped a hatch, and cold air flooded into the hold. "Gizz and Cleaver, I may need your help!"

Gizz and Cleaver followed Nuru out through the hatch and onto the roof. They moved around the freighter until they found a wide tangle of crushed metal wrapped around two of the landing legs. Nuru handed Ring-Sol Ambase's lightsaber to Cleaver and said, "Use this."

Cleaver took the weapon and activated its blade in the same instant that Nuru ignited his own blade. While the Jedi and the droid sliced through the metal debris, Gizz used his bare hands to pull away the heavier chunks of metal and flung them clear of the freighter.

"We're clear!" Nuru said. He switched off his lightsaber, Cleaver did the same, and then Nuru motioned for Cleaver and Gizz to climb back inside the freighter. He followed them in but kept the hatch open as he braced himself within its frame. The freighter lifted from the roof, moved over the yawning chasms between the skyscrapers, and angled toward the lab building.

Cleaver and Gizz noticed Nuru standing in the open hatch. Gizz said, "Are you nuts? Get inside already!"

Nuru ignored Gizz. He was too busy focusing on the lab building and waiting for the right moment to jump. And because everyone in the main hold was watching Nuru, they failed to notice the refresher door open or see the clone trooper they called Sharp as he came staggering out, his helmet askew.

Cad Bane and Robonino had just finished helping Ambase and Sharp load the escape pod onto the *Corona* when Bane heard the loud whine of an approaching engine. He turned and looked up to see the Suwantek freighter, which was listing toward its starboard side and spewing smoke from one thruster.

"Job's over," Bane said. He sprinted for his dropship. Robonino chased after him.

Ambase saw the Suwantek, then saw the small figure who was braced inside an open hatch.

Nuru.

Ambase heard a loud burst, saw a bright flare race away from the dropship, and realized the Duros bounty hunter had just fired a missile at the incoming freighter.

Nuru saw the missile streaking toward him. He had no reason to doubt that Ring-Sol Ambase was responsible for the attack, and he knew there wasn't any chance for the Suwantek to avoid the missile.

The missile glanced off the freighter's lower hull and detonated, throwing the freighter forward. Nuru lost his grip in the hatch's frame and fell, unaware that Cleaver and the trooper he knew as Sharp were also launched off their feet inside the main hold. Cleaver tumbled through the hatch after Nuru and was immediately followed by the disguised Clawdite.

Nuru's Jedi reflexes kicked in as he fell toward the laboratory building's roof, and he swiftly executed a midair somersault that enabled him to land on his feet. A split-second later, Cleaver, still holding Ring-Sol Ambase's lightsaber, jumped down in front of Nuru. The droid was keenly aware that one of the troopers had followed him out of the hatch, and he sprang forward to catch the falling trooper and absorb his impact. The Suwantek zoomed away from the roof, leaving a smoking trail before it vanished between two skyscrapers.

Nuru saw Cleaver catch the trooper before the two figures rolled across the roof. At the same time, the Telgorn dropship lifted off, rising away rapidly from the rooftop before it tore off across the sky. But the young Jedi was not distracted by the rolling figures or the fleeing dropship. His red eyes were locked on Ambase, who was wearing a Republic Navy admiral's uniform and stood beside the *Corona* with his own gaze fixed on Nuru.

And then Nuru noticed the uniformed clone officer who stood a short distance from Ambase, near a row of rectangular skylights. Because Nuru had spent so much time in close proximity with a group of clone troopers, he no longer saw the clones as entirely identical, so he was very surprised to see that the clone in Ambase's company so strongly resembled one member of Breakout Squad.

He looks exactly like Sharp.

Across the roof, the Clawdite rolled out of Cleaver's protective embrace and realized his helmet was about to come straight off his head. The Clawdite automatically shifted his facial muscles and coloring so he would resemble the clone trooper he'd been impersonating since he'd left the planet Kynachi. The helmet came off his head, and he watched it bounce away across the rooftop, secure in the knowledge that he now looked exactly like Sharp. He pushed himself up to his feet and looked back at Nuru and Ambase.

Near Ambase, the clone trooper designated CT-4012, who had been named Sharp because of his remarkably sharp vision, saw his mirror image and realized that he was looking at an imposter in his own armor. CT-4012's face went red with anger.

Ambase noticed the droid commando who'd landed on the roof. The droid held a familiar-looking lightsaber. The lightsaber was Ambase's own, the one that he had constructed for himself many years earlier.

"I see you have something that doesn't belong to you," Ambase said to the droid. He used the Force to pry the lightsaber from the droid's grip, and the weapon flew toward Ambase.

Ambase's lightsaber was flying when Nuru leaped forward and plucked the weapon in midair. Nuru somersaulted across the roof, and when he came up standing, he had a lightsaber in each hand.

The clone in the Republic Navy officer's uniform pounced on his identical counterpart, and the two began fighting, exchanging kicks and punches. One man grabbed the other, but they both lost their balance. They crashed through a skylight and fell into the building.

As Nuru looked back at Ambase, he thought of his recent dream again and felt a stab of fear. He knew what would happen next. A strong gust of wind swept across the roof. Nuru noticed the clouds churning in the sky behind Ambase. Lightning flashed, brightly illuminating the mirrored windows of a nearby skyscraper that resembled a raised sword. Nuru thought of Veeren's death, and his fear was replaced by fury.

Staring at Nuru, Ambase said, "The lightsabers. Give them to me."

Nuru shook his head. "No, you're a killer."

"I'm no killer," Ambase said. "I'm your Master."

Nuru sensed Cleaver moving to his left and heard someone shout. He couldn't tell whether it came from the Clawdite or the clone who was fighting him.

"I can feel your anger, Nuru," Ambase said. He held out both hands, exposing his palms. "I'm defenseless. It's your move."

Nuru was clutching both lightsabers as tightly as he could, but he was unable to stop Ambase from using the Force to tear the weapons from his hands. The lightsabers landed with loud smacks against Ambase's palms. Ambase ignited both blades.

Nuru did not question that his dream had become a reality, and he expected Ambase was about to attack. But he did not expect Cleaver to leap past him and land in front of Ambase.

Ambase swung his lightsaber at the droid's head. Cleaver ducked and kicked out with one leg, aiming for Ambase's midriff. Ambase dodged the kick and drove the other lightsaber, Nuru's weapon, straight through Cleaver's metal chest. Cleaver's photoreceptors went dark as he fell away from the blade and clattered against the roof.

"No!" Nuru screamed. Using the Force, he yanked his lightsaber out of Ambase's grip. The lightsaber's blade automatically deactivated as it flew toward Nuru. He caught the weapon and ignited its blade.

Still clutching his own weapon, Ambase glanced at the fallen droid commando, then looked at Nuru and said, "Allied with the Separatists, have you?"

Nuru did not feel compelled to explain that Cleaver had been his friend. He bared his teeth as he sprang at Ambase. Their lightsabers met with a loud clash.

Nuru spun and swung his lightsaber low, aiming for Ambase's legs. Ambase blocked the attack and shouted, "What happened to you, Nuru?!"

"What happened to *me*?!" Outraged, Nuru swung his lightsaber again and again, but Ambase blocked each strike with ease.

Ambase said, "I know you came here to steal the pod."

Nuru ducked, and Ambase's blade swept over his head. "Then what's it doing in your ship?"

"To stop you from taking it!" Ambase parried another blow.

"You killed an innocent girl at Bilbringi!"

"I didn't—!"

The duel was interrupted by an engine's loud roar. Nuru had almost forgotten about the Suwantek when he saw it rise up suddenly at the far side of the roof. Still spewing smoke from its damaged thruster, the Suwantek edged up over the roof and came down hard, shattering one of its landing legs. A hatch opened, and Knuckles, Breaker, and Gizz jumped out.

Nuru was about to swing his blade again when Ambase raised one hand and used the Force to knock Nuru off his feet, sending him tumbling toward the approaching troopers. Ambase sprinted to the *Corona*.

Nuru rolled to a stop. Breaker arrived beside him and said, "Commander! Are you—?"

Nuru heard the *Corona*'s engines fire. Still holding his lightsaber, he shoved Breaker aside and ran for Ambase's ship. The *Corona* was just lifting off as Nuru leaped onto its nose. Ambase watched from the cockpit as Nuru drove his lightsaber deep into the hull, and then Nuru swept the blade hard to the side. The *Corona*'s nose exploded, launching Nuru back through the air toward the rooftop.

"I got him!" Gizz shouted a moment before Nuru fell into his arms.

Smoke began to fill the hovering *Corona*'s cockpit as the vessel moved toward the edge of the roof. Ambase coughed at the same moment that the ship began shuddering violently, and his forehead accidentally struck a control console's metal bracket. He popped the cockpit's emergency hatch and leaped back to the roof, holding tight to his lightsaber as he landed just ten meters away from Nuru and the giant who held him. Another explosion tore through the *Corona*, and then the entire ship erupted into a ball of fire, sending flaming bits in all directions. The wreckage fell and crashed on a lower roof.

Gizz lowered Nuru to the rooftop just as Breaker and Knuckles arrived at his side. Ambase turned to face the group, and they saw he had a bloody gash on his forehead. Ambase glared at Nuru and said, "You've destroyed the pod."

"At least I stopped you from taking it."

"When did you stray to the dark side, Nuru? Before or after I became your Master?"

"Dark side?" Nuru shook his head. "What are you talking about?"

"Give me the lightsaber, boy."

Gizz drew his blaster. "Why don't you drop yours, mister?"

Ambase ignited his lightsaber. Gizz fired at the Jedi. Ambase swung his blade at the energy bolt and deflected it into the roof. Nuru said, "Put away your blaster, Gizz. And everyone stand back."

Breaker said, "Commander, we can take him—"

"Stand back," Nuru repeated firmly. Taking a

cautious step toward Ambase, he said, "What makes you think I strayed to the dark side?"

"I know you followed me to Kynachi. I was told you're in league with the Sith. I didn't believe it until now."

"Sith?" Nuru took another step forward. "*Who* told you I'm with the Sith?"

"Come one step closer, and I'll cut you down."

Nuru stood very still. "Who told you?"

"Dooku."

Nuru was stunned. "You trusted Dooku?"

Ambase touched the wound on his forehead. "He wasn't . . . always."

"You're confused. And injured."

Ambase leveled his lightsaber at Nuru. "Do you deny that you sabotaged the ship at Kynachi?"

"Of course, I deny it."

"Then why did you follow me?"

"Because I feared for your life, Master Ambase," Nuru said. "I followed you because I wanted to help you."

"Help me?" Ambase's eyes rolled back, and his lightsaber fell from his hand and rolled away from him before his knees buckled and he collapsed.

Nuru went to Ambase's side. He glanced back at Breaker and said, "Get Quills out here with a med kit. Fast!"

As Breaker ran back to the Suwantek, a small cargo ship descended and touched down on the roof. A few seconds later, a hatch opened on the side of the ship, and Lalo Gunn stepped out. Surprised, Knuckles said, "Gunn? What are you doing here?"

"Got me a new ship on Vaced," Gunn said. "I gave Chatterbox a tracking device to plant on the Suwantek so I could catch up with you." She looked at the Suwantek and said, "What happened to you guys? And where's Chatterbox?"

Before anyone could answer, a skylight window slid aside against the roof. A moment later, a clone wearing a Republic Navy officer's uniform pushed himself up through the skylight and climbed onto the roof. Knuckles looked at the clone and said, "Sharp, what are you doing wearing an officer's uniform?"

Sharp looked at Nuru, who was gently elevating Ambase's head, and then he looked at Knuckles. Sharp took a deep breath. "Before I answer that question, Knuckles, why don't you tell me why a Clawdite was wearing my armor."

Knuckles's mouth fell open. "What Clawdite?"

"The one I landed on when I fell through that skylight," Sharp said. "I'd ask him to explain things for me, but it's too late for that. He's dead."

Ring-Sol Ambase, Harro Kelpura, and Chatterbox were whisked to medical centers at the Jedi Temple. Afterward, Breaker brought Cleaver's parts to a droid-repair station.

The bodies of the Clawdite and the three men adorned with Black Sun tattoos were turned over to Republic Intelligence for identification purposes. An attempt was made to deliver Overseer Umbrag's body to the Skakoan embassy in the Senate District, but the Skakoans didn't want it.

Nuru Kungurama, Breaker, and Knuckles talked with Sharp and Lalo Gunn in an effort to figure out, among other things, how and when the Clawdite had infiltrated Breakout Squad, and also Count Dooku's motives for convincing Ambase that Nuru intended to steal the Chiss escape pod. Four days later, they remained largely baffled.

CHAPTER 9

Five days after his return to Coruscant, Nuru went to meet with his recovering Master.

"May I see Master Ambase now?" Nuru Kungurama asked.

"Of course," said the droid receptionist. "Right this way."

Hovering through the air, the droid led Nuru through the medical facility in the Jedi Temple until they arrived at a private room.

The droid quietly ushered Nuru into the room, where Ring-Sol Ambase was sitting on the edge of a narrow bunk. Ambase had a bandage across his forehead.

Seeing Ambase, the droid said, "You should be lying down."

"You should be going away," Ambase said.

"Really!" The offended droid hovered out of the room.

"Greetings, Master Ambase."

"Greetings, Nuru Kungurama."

"I just visited Master Kelpura. He is feeling much better. I hope you are, too?"

Ambase smiled. "Yes, much better. Thanks to you."

Nuru shook his head. "I don't deserve any special thanks, Master. After all, I did try to . . . well, kill you."

"There *were* extenuating circumstances," Ambase said, "such as the fact that I was trying to kill you at the time." Ambase sighed. "I take it that you've reviewed my report to the Jedi Council?"

"Yes, Master."

"I still don't understand everything that happened. Why would Dooku go to such incredible effort to convince me that you were trying to steal the Chiss escape pod?"

"Unless Dooku tells us himself, there are a lot of things we may never know," Nuru said.

"I was informed about the Clawdite and the three men with Black Sun tattoos. Was Republic Intelligence able to identify their bodies?"

"They're still trying."

Ambase frowned. "I wish I could help you reconstruct details, but . . . I still don't remember leaving Kynachi or arriving at Dooku's castle in the Bogden system." Ambase closed his eyes. "How, Nuru? How could I have been so blind? How did I allow myself to be so . . . manipulated by Dooku?"

"I can only guess, but . . . perhaps because he was once your friend, part of you held some hope that you might trust him again."

Ambase smiled again. "You're wise beyond your years, young one."

Nuru bowed politely. "How soon can you return to duty, Master?"

Ambase looked out the window. "I won't be returning to duty."

"I beg your pardon?"

"I'm leaving the Jedi Order and returning to Kynachi."

"But . . . why?"

Ambase looked back at Nuru. "Even though I don't understand what Dooku and Ventress may have been up to, I can't blame them entirely for what happened to me. I've reviewed your report, too, Nuru, about your meeting with the Chiss Aristocra at Bilbringi Depot. I didn't mean to kill that girl when I returned fire to her ship. But I am responsible for taking her life."

"Master, you didn't know what you were—"

Ambase raised a hand to silence Nuru. "Nuru, forgive me, but this war has taken its toll on me. Despite all my training, I allowed myself to be misled, to lose direction. I gave in to fear and anger. I gave in . . . to the dark side."

"But the dark side didn't take you, Master. You . . . you came back."

Ambase smiled sadly. "Although my memory is foggy about various periods over the past few weeks, I remember every detail of our duel in the Dacho District. I don't like admitting it, but I never felt so alive in my life." He touched the bandage on his forehead. "If I hadn't been wounded, I do believe I would have killed you."

"But you didn't, Master."

"You don't understand, Nuru. I was touched by the dark side of the Force. Part of me *wanted* to cut you down. That is no way for any Jedi to think." Ambase shook his head. "The war is over for me. And so is my life as a Jedi. I have a brother on Kynachi. He has a farm. I hope to find peace there."

"But—"

"And I hope your next Master is a better Jedi than I."

Nuru was so astonished he didn't know what to say. He turned and walked slowly to the doorway.

"May the Force be with you, Nuru Kungurama."

Nuru glanced back to the man seated on the edge of the bunk. "May you find peace, Ring-Sol Ambase."

Nuru felt dazed as he left Ambase's room. Proceeding past the droid receptionist, he made his way to the nearest lift tube. The lift tube's door slid open, and Nuru was surprised to see Breaker and Yoda standing inside.

"Good," Yoda said. "Found you, we have. A meeting with you, Chancellor Palpatine has requested."

"Ah, Nuru Kungurama," Supreme Chancellor Palpatine said, smiling as he stepped away from the broad desk in his office in the Senate Office Building. "At last we meet in person."

Standing beside Yoda and Breaker, Nuru bowed politely. Nuru casually surveyed the office. Behind Palpatine's desk, a wide window offered a sweeping view of the air traffic that moved in neat paths across Galactic City's skyline. Although sunlight poured in through the window, the office's red-painted walls were so strangely dark that Nuru had to blink a few times to adjust his vision.

Palpatine came to a stop in front of Nuru and said, "I just wanted to thank you personally for everything you've done for the Republic."

"You give me too much credit, Chancellor." Nuru gestured to Breaker. "If not for the other members of Breakout Squad, I never would have survived the mission to Kynachi."

"Ah, the modesty of a Jedi." Palpatine smiled again. "I hope the Jedi Council appreciates your efforts. While I understand why the Council may have had misgivings about letting such a young

Padawan lead a series of missions, I believe your accomplishments speak for themselves. I commend you *and* Breakout Squad."

Yoda remained silent. Nuru said, "Thank you, Chancellor."

Palpatine looked to Yoda. "Master Yoda, at this time in history, every Jedi capable of leading troops is a great asset to the Republic. And I think you'll agree that if we're to defeat the Separatists, we need all the help we can get. Nuru Kungurama and his squad have already proven most resourceful."

Yoda narrowed his eyes as he glanced at Nuru and muttered, "Hrmm."

Still facing Yoda, Palpatine said, "I would never ask you or the Council to consider allowing just any young Padawan to lead missions, but Nuru Kungurama is not just any young Padawan. Circumstances have given him invaluable experience, the very kind of experience we need to preserve the Republic."

Before Yoda could respond, Nuru said, "I do appreciate your confidence in Breakout Squad, Chancellor, but I think you overestimate my abilities."

Palpatine looked at Nuru. "You really are too modest. If you had the Council's permission, you *would* continue to lead Breakout Squad, yes?"

"Yes, Chancellor."

Returning his attention to Yoda, Palpatine said, "The Kynachi government requires military support to transport starship technology to our new facility at Bilbringi. Breakout Squad is familiar with the routes between those systems. Unless another Jedi is available to lead Breakout Squad, perhaps Nuru Kungurama could do this?"

Yoda frowned. "Discuss this with the Council, I will."

"Thank you, Master Yoda," Palpatine said. "I admit, I was reluctant to ask for your help in this matter, but these are extraordinary times, and we are at war."

Yoda and Nuru bowed to Palpatine, then Breaker followed the two Jedi out of the office. After his visitors had left, Palpatine went through a door that led to a smaller meeting room. He looked to a high-backed chair, on which a girl was seated. The girl had blue skin, red eyes, and gleaming, black hair.

"I apologize for that interruption, Aristocra Sev'eere'nuruodo," Palpatine said. "I appreciate your patience."

"I cannot remain here much longer."

Palpatine frowned. "But we have so much to discuss. If our governments are to form an alliance—"

"The Chiss Ascendancy is *considering* an alliance."

"Yes, of course," Palpatine said. "Might we at least finish what we were discussing? You said you suspected there might be a conspiracy to conquer the Galactic Republic?"

"I did."

Keeping his eyes fixed on Veeren, Palpatine lowered his voice as he said, "You don't really believe that, do you, Aristocra?"

Veeren blinked. "No. Not anymore." She rose from her chair.

"Aristocra, before you leave, I hope you might enlighten me about something. The Jedi Council allowed me to review Nuru Kungurama's report of his last sighting of you at Bilbringi. He remains under the impression that he saw your ship explode and that you were killed."

"As I have already explained, an approaching ship fired at mine at Bilbringi. I deemed it necessary to leave no trace of my presence there. I detonated the outermost shell of my ship's hull to distract the attacker, and at the same time made what you might call a micro-jump into hyperspace so no one could follow me."

"So you told me, but what I don't understand is . . . why do you wish for Nuru Kungurama to continue believing you are dead? And why trust me with that secret?"

"Because I have my reasons," Veeren said. "At least for now."

"If that is your wish, so be it. But when might you and I have another discussion about an alliance?"

"Perhaps after your Civil War is over. Now, I must return to the Chiss Ascendancy."

Palpatine bowed deeply. "Until we meet again, Aristocra." When he rose, he saw Aristocra Sev'eere'nuruodo was already walking straight for the door that led to the private lift tube that would deliver her to her waiting starship. She entered the lift tube, and the door hissed closed behind her.

Knuckles, Sharp, and a newly refurbished Cleaver were in the clone trooper barracks, their eyes riveted to a holovid report. The projection of the female Rodian reporter's image vanished, but her voice continued to speak as her image was replaced by a group of Mandalorian guards examining an empty display cabinet.

"But the Mandalorian government has reported the theft of a suit of Mandalorian armor from the Sundari Peace Museum three days ago, the same day a MandalMotors Pursuer-class enforcement ship went missing from the Sundari shipping docks. An investigation by Mandalorian authorities has determined that both the armor and ship were stolen by a Corellian bounty hunter named Ranno Task, whose remains were positively identified on Vaced one hour ago. In other HoloNet News . . ."

Knuckles switched off the holovid. "I guess that settles it."

"What settles what?" Lalo Gunn said as she entered the barracks with Chatterbox. Chatterbox was wearing lightweight pants with a matching shirt that covered the bacta patches on his torso.

Knuckles said, "The Mandalorians had nothing to do with that guy we ran into on Vaced. Still, that guy was a tough fighter, huh, Sharp?"

Sharp rolled his eyes. "For the last time, Breaker . . . I've never been to Vaced. Or to Chiss space. Or tangled with the Black Hole Pirates. You keep confusing me with the Clawdite."

"Well," Knuckles said, "when you think about everything that happened, it *is* kind of confusing."

"*I'm* not confused," Cleaver said. "I knew there was something odd about that trooper. When he shot Overseer Umbrag, I realized he moved remarkably faster than clone troopers."

Gunn said, "Chatterbox and I were almost certain there was something wrong with Sharp." She looked at Sharp and added, "I meant the Clawdite. No offense."

"None taken."

Knuckles said, "Gunn, I still don't get it. The Duros bounty hunter hired you to take us off Kynachi and also fly us to Vaced?"

"Yeah, and he paid pretty well, too. But after we started suspecting there was a saboteur on board the *Harpy*, I told Chatterbox about the Duros hiring me, and we decided to find out if the Duros had planted a saboteur."

Knuckles glared at Chatterbox. "You couldn't have let your pals in on this secret?"

Chatterbox shrugged.

Gunn continued, "We didn't tell anyone else, Knucklehead, because we wanted to *catch* the saboteur, not scare him off. But all I found out from the Duros was that he sent Robonino to the Black Hole sector to infiltrate the McGrrrr Gang and prevent the pirates from harming anyone on the *Harpy*."

"But *why*?" Knuckles said.

Gunn scowled. "Remind me to ask the Duros next time I see him. Anyway, when all of you were at Bilbringi Depot, Chatterbox also noticed Sharp—I mean the Clawdite—moved faster than any clone. Unfortunately, Chatterbox wasn't able to tell you that before he got shot."

Gizz lumbered into the barracks, carrying a large container. "Hey, guys. I picked up some food for everybody."

Suspicious, Knuckles said, "Where'd you get the food, Gizz?"

Gizz beamed as he placed the container on a table. "A waitress in Co-Co Town gave it to me. She said not to come back to her diner until after I took a bath. Lucky day! Who wants ribs?"

Before anyone could answer, Nuru and Breaker entered the barracks. Nuru smiled as he looked at his allies and said, "I'm glad to see you up and walking, Chatterbox. And, Cleaver, you're looking much better, too."

"Thank you, Commander Nuru," Cleaver said. "How is Master Ambase?"

The question caught Nuru off guard, but he managed to respond, "He's doing . . . well."

Sharp said, "How did your meeting go with Palpatine?"

Breaker said, "The Chancellor wants Nuru to continue leading Breakout Squad."

"That's terrific!" Knuckles said. "Next time the Chancellor's up for election, he'll have my vote."

Nuru said, "My future really is the Jedi Council's decision. We'll just have to wait and see what happens. Personally, I don't expect—"

Nuru was interrupted by his own loudly chirping holocomm unit. He took the device from his belt, pressed a button, and a small hologram of Yoda appeared above his hand. "Yes, Master Yoda?"

"A mission for you and Breakout Squad, we have," Yoda said. "A freighter, the *Spice Siren*, has gone missing in the Tatooine system. An act of piracy, we suspect."

Nuru was surprised. He had not expected another mission so soon. He said, "Master Yoda, may I ask . . . is there a reason you want Breakout Squad for this assignment?"

"Carrying munitions for the Republic, the freighter was. A secret mission, this is. And experience with such missions, you have."

"I understand. We'll leave at once."

"May the Force be with you, *Commander* Nuru." Yoda's hologram flickered out.

Knuckles said, "We're back in action!"

"I'll bring the ribs," Gizz said.

Gunn said, "Where's Chatterbox?"

A moment later, Chatterbox emerged wearing his armor and carrying a blaster rifle. He said, "Let's go."

THE END